ANGEL'S GUARDIAN

ANGEL'S GUARDIAN

SHARON LYNN HODGE

Eloquent Books
Durham, Connecticut

Eloquent Books
An imprint of Strategic Book Group
P. O. Box 333
Durham, CT 06422
http://www.StrategicBookGroup.com

ISBN: 978-1-60911-933-1

Book Design by Julius Kiskis

Printed in the United States of America
18 17 16 15 14 13 12 11 10   1 2 3 4 5

DEDICATION

I dedicate this book to the one person who won my heart and
handed me a pen with hope and inspiration for me to write
once more.
With all the love and appreciation one heart can give to
another,
"Thank you!" Brian W Graft!

I extend a special note of thanks to Eva Ice for her assistance
with editing and proofing my manuscript.
"Thank you!" to Eva, Kathy, Topsy, and Jaclyn, for being my
greatest and first fan club!

INTRODUCTION

A little girl played quietly in a sandbox at the edge of a playground. It was a quiet afternoon, only half a dozen children were at the park playground. It was hot for September but a gentle breeze turned her blonde tresses to shimmering gold in the suns brilliance. Lilting vocals sang children's songs, emanating from her small mouth and carried by the breeze to her mother's ears. A soft smile spread across the woman's face as she listened to her child at play, then she focused on the novel in her hands.

Dense brush hid a man from their view where he crouched just behind the blonde haired, blue-eyed child that sat in the sandbox singing. Sweat dripped from his face onto his camouflage shirt as he waited patiently for just the right moment. Carefully, he observed the children and their mothers, especially the mother of the little blonde haired, blue-eyed beauty that sat just six feet away from him. He knew she was the designated child he was to kidnap from the snapshot of her in his hand. Tucking it back into his pocket, he prepared to make his move.

He did not have to wait much longer. Within a few moments, the other children were huddled with their parents for a snack and drink. The little ones mother was distracted for a moment as she watched the children scramble for their drinks and food. He leapt forward, covered her mouth with his large hand and within seconds, melted into the woods unnoticed with the little angelic looking girl. Following instructions, he took the girl to a hunting cabin deep in the mountains of Center County Pennsylvania and locked her in a large dog kennel. He had removed her clothes and placed them in a small garbage bag.

It was hot and stuffy in the cabin; however, a thin blanket and a bottle of water had been left in the cage for her. Guilt washed over him as heart wrenching sobs racked the young girl's body. He wondered what his brother had in store for the girl and he almost took her out of the cage and back to the park. He wanted no part of hurting a child, but he desperately needed the money promised him for his participation in the kidnapping. Besides, his brother had promised that he did not intend to harm the girl.

Locking several deadbolts on the cabin door as he left, he hesitated once more as the final lock slid into place. A look of sheer determination replaced the indecision on his face and with his jaw firmly set, he strode to his truck. Firing it up, he floored the gas pedal, slinging gravel and dust into the air as he peeled out of the driveway. Truck bouncing wildly, he drove to the site deep in the woods where he was to meet his brother at dusk. He parked his truck, removed a cooler of beer and ice, and settled in for the long wait until dusk.

Just as the stars began to twinkle in the sky he heard his brothers vehicle approaching. Lifting the flask in his right hand, he drained the last swallow of Jack Daniels and chased it with a half a bottle of cold beer. Staggering to his feet just as his brother pulled up and parked, he picked up the bag with the girls clothing and threw it to him.

"Where's my money at?" he slurred to the man getting out

of the vehicle.

"It's already here bro; I hid it in the woods so I wouldn't have to carry it to work."

"Well give it up so I can be dun with this messy shit!"

"Okay, okay. Is the girl where I told you to put her?"

"Yep, all locked up like a fucking dog, just the way you ordered! You got a sick mind bro."

"Yeah, yeah, whatever you say drunk! Whatever you say. Let's go get your money" the man replied as he strode towards a path into the woods. In a drunken stupor, the kidnapper followed behind him, completely unaware of the gun hidden under his brother's coat. A ways into the woods the brush became much thicker and at a large oak tree the brother with the gun stopped.

"It's right there, in the hollow at the fork in the tree," he informed the drunken man. As the kidnapper reached up to retrieve the reward for his dastardly deed, a gunshot exploded through the quiet night. The man fell against the tree and slid to the ground, realizing a second before the shot that the hollow in the tree was empty. His reward was a bullet to his leg, slicing through the femoral artery. Within minutes, he took his last breath and after removing the snapshot of the girl-child from the dead mans coat, he covered the body with leaves and brush. The murdered kidnapper would remain hidden there through the bitter winter, until the spring thaw.

In the valley down below, a little girl sat in a dog kennel, tears still running down her face, heart aching for her mother. The gunshot startled her as it broke the singing of the crickets in the velvety black place where she was caged. A deathly quiet fell over the cabin and Angel could hear herself breathing rapidly in the darkness, her heart fluttering with fear in her chest. Then, out of nowhere, a sudden peaceful feeling washed over her, comforting her soul. She heard a rustling in the rafters above her but did not jump with fear.

"Hush little one, do not be afraid. Close your eyes and think of your mother. I am your guardian angel and I am here to help you." The voice was so low she could not be sure she had even heard the words with her ears. It was if they came from inside of her head, but the comforting they brought to her anguished soul was real. Angel wrapped herself in the threadbare blanket left for her and curled up on the hard cage floor. Soon she was fast asleep, dreams of her mother were dancing in her mind, dispelling the nightmare she had just found herself living in...

PART 1

VANISHING ANGEL

CHAPTER 1

Alone, the woman sat on the park bench amid throngs of sun-drenched Labor Day picnickers soaking up the last of the hot summer rays. Children's squeals and the laughter of families mingled with delightful smells emanating from strategically placed grills throughout the park. Her lowered eyes and clenched hands hidden in a windbreaker on her lap were the only outward signs of the agony tearing through her soul.

"Why" she screamed silently, "who are you and what have you done with my child?"

A tear slid down her pretty face, bruised behind the sunglasses and make-up, and she angrily swiped it away, frustrated at her own weakness. Robert hated her crying, as was evidenced by her bluish purple skin under dark glasses and make-up. The muscles that ached stiffly when she adjusted her slight frame on the hard park bench also bore testimony to his incredibly short temper. Physical pain was drowned out however by the incredible waves of emotional agony that eroded her sanity and threatened to drive her over the edge of reason.

"Where is she?" her mind screamed as her arms ached for her little girl. Flashbacks of the beautiful angelic child played relentlessly through her mind, so vivid were the images she could almost feel and smell her right there in her arms. Taking a deep breath and lifting her chin she pulled herself from the brink of madness, determined anew to find her little Angel.

Desperate dark blue eyes again searched children's faces as they laughed and played, praying silently that she would find that one familiar face. Her daughters face, her one and only daughter and the youngest of three children. Her boys were grown and out on their own by the time Rebecca's little Angel was four years old. Angel was her life, her reason for living and breathing and now she had vanished. In a split second, a glitch in time, so small she still could not comprehend how it had happened, her little Angel was gone.

As the sun began to set, Rebecca walked the park one last time. Twilight and relentless mosquito's eventually chased off the last of the park guests and she found herself all alone in the near dark. Hope turned to despair once more with the waning daylight as she climbed into her mini-van for the return home, back to Robert's short fuse and third degree about where she had been. The press would probably be camped in there front yard yet and the cops would probably have even more questions for them again. The past four days, since her little Angel had vanished, were endless hours filled with questions and demands, confusion and anxiety, and worst of all the intense pain and incredible loneliness. Also were the ever-intensifying bouts of Robert's temper.

She hoped the police would not notice the purpling flesh under the rim of her dark shades. She had done her best to cover them up. The last thing she wanted to do right now was discuss her fiancé's need of late to vent his anger on her slender frame and pretty face. Eleven months they had been together now. There had been good times, full of laughter, lovemaking, and wonderful memories. The last several months seemed like a web of nightmares that had devoured her soul, her life, her hope, and her love for Robert.

The nightmare had begun after returning home late in the evening from a night of drinking and dancing at a local nightclub. She had been driving that stormy night and had accidentally hit a trashcan that had blown into the driveway. His punishment for her mistake came crashing down upon her in excruciating bouts of blows to her face and sharp kicks to her ribs, stomach, arms and legs. He became a monster before her very eyes and as quickly as it started, it ended. Rebecca's body, balled up tightly in the fetal position in an attempt to protect her from his vicious blows, lay on the cold garage floor. After he left the garage and she was sure he was not returning, she picked herself up off the floor grimacing with the pain and her mind in a daze. She could not comprehend what he had just done to her, or why.

Robert had torn her heart apart that night, for each name that he had called her cut deep into her heart like a knife. However, when she awoke the next morning, he was sitting in a chair beside her bed where he claimed to have been sitting for hours. He pulled her to him and whispered apologies and promises to salve the wounds on her heart until she relented and forgave him.

Thus, the nightmare began, and she lived in that nightmarish state since that opening night on the stage of abuse on which so many women find themselves. She was unable to awake from the nightmare, so she had adjusted her life to accommodate it. She decided, for the time being that she loved him deeply and could not fathom going on in life without him.

CHAPTER 2

Persistent ringing penetrated the heavy drug induced fog of sleep that blanketed the young woman asleep on the sofa.

"Hello" spoke her husky sleepy voice after several moments.

"Ms. Watts?" questioned a deep male voice from the receiver.

"Yes? Who is calling?" queried Rebecca, stifling a yawn.

"Ms. Watts, I was wondering if my partner and I could stop by and speak to you?' asked Detective Howell.

"Now?" she replied glancing at the wall clock, "it's six o-clock in the morning!"

"I know" he replied sympathetically, "but this is a matter of grave importance," and he flinched involuntarily at his unintentional play on words.

"O.K.' Rebecca conceded, fear beginning to trickle into the awakening cells of her mind and her heart beginning to hammering against her ribs.

Hanging up the receiver, she rose from her makeshift bed and stumbled sleepily into the bathroom where she washed the fog of sleep away with cold water and a shot of Listerine. Rebecca's heart however only beat faster with the fogginess of sleep scattered and the dawning of realization seeping into her now wide-awake brain cells. Whatever it was that the police wanted she knew it could not be any good news at six a.m.

6

"Might as well start a pot of coffee," she mumbled to herself. Robert would be up soon and would be irritated because she had spent the night on the couch after their spat the night before. Reaching for the coffee, the sleeve of her robe slid back to reveal a now purpling forearm, bearing evidence of her trauma the night before at Robert s hands.

"Damn" she mumbled, "I'll have to remember to keep my sleeves down while the detectives are here. "Oh well" she sighed silently, "I'm getting all to used to hiding these bruises." With her little Angel still missing, the very thought of leaving Robert brought such loneliness and despair that she would not even consider the reality of it.

Much sooner than she expected the door bell buzzed and coffee splashed from her mug to the kitchen floor as the sound jolted her from the depths of her agonizing thoughts. "Had they found her little girl? Was she dead or alive? and, Oh God, had she been hurt or molested?" ran through her mind with such force she couldn't breath. Her hands shook so violently that she had to put her mug down to open the door.

Sympathy etched the faces of the officers, evident in the light of the developing dawn, and

Rebecca's heart plummeted to despair. Knees gave way, legs buckled, and black despair flicked the last light of consciousness from her eyes. The female officer stepped forward and caught her before physical injury could be added to the mental anguish that was crushing the beautiful young mother she held gently in her arms.

The news they had to break to her would only push the woman further towards the edge of insanity. The middle-aged female officer had raised three children of her own, two of whom were successful young women now. Just the thought of losing one of them shot a sudden stab of fear through her very soul. Sarah gently eased the woman down to the floor as her partner, Tyler, grabbed a pillow from the couch and placed it under Rebecca's head. Assured of a strong, although rapid pulse, Sarah gently rubbed the woman's hands and softly called her name.

Rebecca stirred and consciousness slowly invaded the black veil that had drawn over her mind. Blinking slowly, Rebecca's mind sluggishly fought to return to full consciousness.

"What was it?" her mind reached out, questioning, probing gently at the memory center of her brain. She gasped suddenly, having retrieved the memory that had caused the sudden closing down of her body and mind. Her eyes flew open and panic and fear filled the dark blue orbs that were now searching Sarah's face for answers.

Empathetically, Sarah helped the woman to her feet and over to the sofa where she eased her back to lie down until she recovered. God knew that the words she had to expose the woman's already raw and tortured soul and she ached in her own heart for the pain she must inflict.

"We need you to come to the station, Rebecca." Sarah said softly. Tortured eyes bored into hers, unspoken questions behind the red-rimmed pools of pain. Rebecca simply nodded her assent, as words were impossible for her to speak now. Her larynx was frozen with the fear of what they needed to reveal to her.

"What's going on here?" an irritated male voice suddenly reverberated from a landing above the living room stairs. "Who are you people and what are you all doing in my home at this hour of the day?" he asked, addressing the two plains clothes investigators. Investigator Tyler cleared his throat gruffly and then patiently explained to an irate Robert the purpose of their untimely visit and therefore, their invasion of his home.

"We need to have Rebecca come down to the station with us" Sarah spoke firmly. "We need to ask her a few more questions."

"What could you possibly have to ask us that you haven't already covered?" he snapped back at her. "It's fucking six in the morning! Couldn't you have at least waited until a decent hour to interrogate us further?"

"This is of grave importance," Sarah said softly but authoritatively, "and we don't need you to accompany us." She made a mental note of his extreme agitation over having to be interrogated further. It seemed to her the least he could do was cooperate with the investigation to find the missing girl.

"Like hell she's going there alone!" he snarled back. "There is nothing you need to question her about without my being present." Sarah noted the sudden tension in Rebecca face and way her hand suddenly tightened around her own. Tyler broke in and forcefully informed the man on the landing of exactly their intent.

"Mr. Wilson, you are more than welcome to accompany us to the station and wait there while we talk to your fiancé, however, there are things we need to discuss alone with her concerning her daughter." Mumbling obscenities, Robert strode away and disappeared from sight, a slamming door moments later informing them of his opinion of the matter. Tyler Howell made a mental note to run another background check on Mr. Robert Wilson. Simultaneously, his partner, Sarah Kovach, made a mental note to double check on Roberts alibi for the day of the day of Angel's disappearance. Something about the man needled at the investigators and made them want to take a second look at him.

CHAPTER 3

Gray green cement block walls built in a twelve by sixteen rectangle was what greeted Rebecca at the station. Cold fluorescent lights burned starkly overhead and a long stainless steel table winked coldly at her as she sat down in a metal chair bolted to a cement floor. The sterility of the room frightened her, reminding her of the operating rooms she had worked in during her seven-year employment at Cheltenham Memorial Hospital assisting pediatric brain surgeon, Dr. Gene Macon.

A chill ran up her spine as she flashed back to the harshness of the surgery. It was the way the surgeons sawed the skull in two and then popped the top off like a mushroom from its stem. Rebecca always did avoid directly viewing the exposed intellectual matter. As much blood, exposed flesh, and organs as she had seen, her gag reflex asserted itself as ruler during this one procedure. Nervous, she glanced around the small cubicle and noted a dark tinted window built into the wall in front of her. Doubtless, she would be observed by several pairs of eyes from the other side of the black square, just as they did at the surgical center with the interns. Only these would be detectives trained to observe and determine whether one was telling the truth or covering up some terrible crime. Swallowing hard, blinking rapidly to stem the flow of tears, and threatening tendrils of fear, she waited silently for whatever tragedy it was that caused them to bring her in...

After a slight tap on the door, it opened to reveal a nerdy looking young man with heavy rimmed black glasses carrying a small cardboard box. Behind him, she saw Sarah and for an instant felt some slight relief at seeing the familiar and usually friendly face. The thin pimple faced man placed the box on the table and abruptly left the room, Sarah took a seat directly across from Rebecca and as blue eyes met gray an understanding seemed to pass quietly between them. This would not be an easy meeting, something dark and painful lie between them in the shape of the cardboard box.

"Rebecca," the woman started "this is the hardest thing I've ever had to do in my twelve years as a detective on the Homicide Force. I cannot begin to fathom your anguish and fear, but I must do this for Angel's sake, and yours." She mentally noted the expressions on the young woman's face. There was no guilt or conscious anxiety mirrored in the woman's face, only deep anguish and raw fear. At that moment, Sarah mentally crossed Rebecca off her list of possible suspects. This woman in front of her showed only the pain of a mother's loss of a dear child.

Slowly, the investigator opened the box and an audible gasp escaped from Rebecca's mouth as a plastic Ziploc bag with a pink Myrtle Beach tee shirt was exposed. A strangled sob arose from deep with-in the mother's soul as her violently trembling hands reached for the remnants of her child. Sarah gently took the woman's hands before they could touch the evidence within and gently explained why she could not touch them.

Rebecca wanted to take the tiny shirt in her hands, bury her face in the soft cotton, and breathe in her little Angel's scent that would have lingered behind in the fabric. Little did she know those Angelic smells had vanished days ago wiped away eternally by both natures, and mans, harsh elements. With-in its folds, the shirt held secret horrors that no mother should have to know, and for now, at least they did not speak. Rebecca would not know for quite some time what secrets the little tee shirt had to reveal.

Sarah knew by the intense reaction of the woman in front of her two things for sure. One, she had had nothing to do with the disappearance of her daughter and two, the shirt in the box definitely belonged to little Angel Lee-Anne Watts. Gently she placed a comforting arm around the woman's quaking shoulders and led her from the room and down the hall. Entering a more comfortable room with padded chairs, soft light and refreshing drinks she placed a cup of cold water in trembling hand. She avoided the panicked dark blue orbs that pierced her brown ones with a thousand questions. They were questions that Sarah had few answers for now.

Very little evidence had presented itself as of yet, only the pink cotton shirt and a single solitary tiny sock had turned up in the woods around the park. Grid searches had been conducted several times and absolutely no shred of evidence was missed, of that, she was certain. So where was little Angel? Why were her shirt and a sock lying abandoned in the woods all by their lonesome? Most importantly, who was responsible for this atrocious tragedy? Sorting through her thoughts, she escorted Rebecca to the undercover cruiser and drove her back to her home.

CHAPTER 4

Rebecca's hands trembled as she put the key in the lock and opened the door to Robert and her home. Eyes searched the home to find the object of her love, and her apprehension. Wearily she sank onto the couch where her pillow and blanket still lay from her episode of unconsciousness. Robert must have left or gone back to bed. Her eyes closed quickly, eyelids fluttering only two or three times, before she sank into the sleep of sheer exhaustion. She dreamed of a golden haired blue-eyed little girl dancing on the lush green grass of the park. A smile played across her full lips and a slight smile parted them briefly.

He stood there looking down at his beautiful wife to be and a smile played across his mouth, softening the hard lines of his face for a moment. Robert was a handsome man. At fifty-one he was still firm and fit, flat cut abs, muscled arms, and solid legs resulted from the five days a week he spent working out at the local gym. His jet-black hair was sprinkled with gray and crows feet had cropped up around his dark brown eyes gave awry some of his true age. In a dimly lit room or club however, he could still pass for a much younger man. Now he stood over his future wife and his thoughts were dual. Part of him loved her constantly, wanted to possess her completely, the other half of his soul loathed her and her weaknesses.

Robert s mother had been a strong woman in constant control of her husband, five children two girls, and three boys.

Robert had been the youngest of the clan and thus he had been coddled and pampered by his mother until he became a young man. It was then that he was drafted to fight in Viet Nam and forced to face reality and become a man. Ever since then he had despised weakness of any kind in the human race.

He loved his mother but hated the way she had pampered him for her own selfish desires. The weak must be forced, as he had been, to become strong; or otherwise be exterminated from the human race in order to make way for the strong. Survival of the fittest, was not that how the very world carne into existence? Robert believed that God himself had visited him on that battlefield in Viet Nam and commanded him to "go forth and destroy the weak that were shaming Him and His creation." But he was to do it quietly and secretly, it was his mission from the man upstairs. Ever since 1969 upon his return from Nam' Robert had been secretly conducting experiments on people he found to be weak and spineless, the majority of which he found on the streets. The weakest and most spineless of living beings, the dregs of humanity he preyed upon for his specimens. He now had boxes and boxes of notes detailing his secret lab experiments in his hidden lab. Rebecca was to have been one of those experiments, one of the few he had gleaned from everyday middle classed people.

Something about her, however, had not allowed him to hurt her. In spite of her weaknesses, he found himself drawn to her and the strong attributes she did have. Thus, she had escaped his "chamber of strength" as Robert called it. Deep in the mountains of Clinton County, Pennsylvania, stood a log cabin and behind its walls, unspeakable acts of horror had taken place. Every one of them had been captured on videotape and handwritten notes in hundreds of notebooks. He also kept a daily journal in which he had recorded his deepest thoughts and feelings about his mission.

Watching the sleeping woman, he let his thoughts drift to the child that was now lying on the floor of a dog cage awaiting his "chamber." She was the youngest of all his experiments yet, and promised to be the most successful. The thought of her lying on his table, cries of learning truth and strength filling the air around him drove to a heightened sense of arousal. His heart started to pound and adrenalin rushed through his body at the mere thought of her. He would make her his greatest success of all. The whiny little seven-year-old brat would turn out to be the toughest bitch or she would die like all the other weak spineless saps that lay buried in the mountains of Clinton County.

"A graveyard of weaklings" he thought to himself as a cruel light glinted in his eyes and another rush of adrenalin shot through his body. He closed his eyes and let it wash over him, driving him into an even more heightened state of arousal. His cock started to get hard and he looked down at the woman lying in front of him. He needed release and she would have to suffice for now.

Kneeling in front of her, he leaned in and kissed her roughly, firmly squeezing her left breast, awakening her from her troubled sleep. Rebecca woke slowly, feeling Robert's hand painfully squeezing her breast and a silent groan went through her mind. She would not refuse him, could not refuse him. He would take what he wanted from her anyway even if she did, so she slipped into automatic pilot as she had learned to do lately.

"Suck me baby," he growled in her ear as he reached down to unzip his pants.

"Suck me hard, just like I taught you to do."

He shoved his hardened penis at her soft full lips and she opened her mouth and took him in, her stomach lurching wildly as she fought down the bile rising in her throat. She sucked him the way he taught her, slow and hard, and she felt him tense. Within moments, his breath became ragged and his cock throbbed, warning of the impending mouth full of cum. She let her mind drift away so she could take it without retching and thus making him furious.

"Oh you sexy bitch, God you're so good, soooo good my sexy little bitch" his mind drifting to the little girl in the cage at his cabin.

"Ahhhhhhhhhh" he groaned as he let his ample offering loose in her soft willing mouth. He felt her swallow his seed as the last spasms of ecstasy jerked through his body and he pulled his cock slowly out of her mouth. She lay there devastated and nauseated, stomach threatening to rid itself of the salty fluid that it did not want. Tears pricked her eyes and her throat clenched with silent sobs as she rolled over and faced. the back of the couch.

CHAPTER 5

The tiny figure covered with a threadbare blanket shivered within the confines of a large metal dog cage. Wind howled through cracks in the log walls of a tiny cabin stirring dust devils in dim orange light emanating from a rusty pot bellied stove in the middle of the two-room shack. Outside, frost glistened on the grass; caught in the moons cold stare while a wisp of smoke drifted eerily into the gray-purple sky of predawn.

Angel shivered and tried to curl into a tighter ball to keep her teeth from chattering. She heard gravel crunching under tires of an approaching vehicle and moments later the front door opened and then slammed shut amidst a blast of cold air. Heavy footsteps sounded across old floorboards and made their way to the old stove. A hand reached out and shook the grate handle blowing ash dust thickly into the air from holes rusted through the belly of the stove causing Angel to cough and then sneeze quite abruptly. The man glanced over at her briefly and then opened the door of the stove and made eerie shadows on the ceilings and walls of the shack. Angel's now wide open eyes took in the quaking shadows and flickering light and watched as the man threw wood and large black rocks into the iron stove.

Coal dust made the fire catch and roar and the warmth bathed her. Within minutes her teeth stopped chattering she stayed very still however, afraid to anger the man as she had made that mistake several times already. He was cruel and what her momma had taught her was a very bad man. He hurt her badly but she tried very hard not to scream or cry anymore. Four weeks seemed like four years since she had been brought to this horrid place... The ugly hateful things he had done caused her to retreat from current time and the present world into a quiet safe place in her own mind where she felt little pain.

Self-preservation pushed her mind and soul to that quiet retreat away from her attacker. Robert thought she was weak; however, Angel was a lot tougher than he realized and in time, he would discover just how tough she really was. The stubbornness born of tragedy already experienced by little Angel would carry through and see her to the end of her nightmare. Nevertheless, what a nightmare it would play out to be! Unspeakable horrors would be heaped on her tiny soul in the future, and in the moments to come.

Suddenly, the man came to her, opened the cage and snatched the sheet from her thin frame. Angel gasped as cool air struck her finally warm skin. He grabbed her by the dog collar around her neck and lifted her roughly to her feet. Trembling, she stood before him, half-naked, terror oozing from every pore of her body. Glancing quickly at his face, she knew it was Robert again, as usual. The man who had kidnapped her never came back to take her back to her mother. Robert was being especially nasty today. Adrenaline rushed through his body, as he smelled her terror. He could not get over how the smell of terror turned him on! It was the greatest high in the world, the finest drug, and he had tried them all on himself and his experiments. He took a deep breath taking in her terror scent and letting the rush flow through his body. His eyes perused her beautiful little body and he felt desire growing in his loins, but he steeled himself against his growing desire.

"Not yet" he said to himself between clenched teeth. "I'll make you mine when the time is right and you have grown as strong as me." He grabbed the dog chain attached to the collar and half dragged her to a rickety old table in the corner where he pushed her into an equally rickety chair. He observed tears welling up in his eyes and felt disappointed. She should be learning by now.

"What a weak little bitch you are" he said cruelly. "You will be my tough little bitch one day, just you wait and see." Grabbing a dirty skillet from a washtub, he slammed it onto an ugly green rusty cook stove. The sound made Angel jump. From a cooler he extricated a carton of eggs and a stick of butter.

"Got to keep your strength up my dear" he addressed to Angel. "You'll be here a long time and you have a lot of lessons you need to be taught."

Angel's stomach rumbled. The first few days she was in captivity she had refused to eat anything. Eventually survival took over and she ignored the unsanitary conditions and ate heartily of the food he prepared. She was extremely hungry after the long cold night on the hard floor of the cage.

Eggs sizzled in the dirty frying pan and her mouth watered, she did not care about the dirt anymore, she just wanted to eat. Moments later, he threw a paper plate in front of her with a stale piece of bread and half-raw eggs. Angel wolfed them down within minutes. They barely satiated her appetite, but it was better than nothing was. After eating, she had to go to the bathroom, so she made her way to a plastic bucket with a makeshift wooden seat in the corner. The seat gave her splinters but she had to go very bad. The man was watching her and her little face flushed with embarrassment as she did her business in the makeshift potty then wiped. Her heart began to hammer under his scrutinizing glare it was time for "lessons" as the man called them.

The lessons were about pain, always. Each time he hurt her she vowed she would not cry. Crying seemed to anger him and make him hurt her more. Eventually he always won and her screams would enrage him so that he would leave, and then she would be all alone. She was scared of that too. What if he never came back to take care of her? She would die all alone in the doggy cage of thirst and starvation. She missed her mother terribly. She cried herself to sleep each night thinking of her momma.

She could see her face in her mind and smell her perfume almost as if she was holding her in her arms. Angel burned those memories into her mind to keep with her always. She did not know why her step-dad was doing the things to her that he was because he had never hurt her that way before. Robert had a temper and angered easily but he was usually very nice to her, until he had kidnapped her that is. She did not like the way he had started hitting her mother either but he had never hit her.

CHAPTER 6

Sarah Kovach sat morosely at her desk, her mind weighing heavily on Rebecca and a petite little girl named Angel. She had just hung up the phone after speaking with Rebecca, who still called frequent to inquire on the case concerning her daughter. Months had passed since Angel's disappearance and still no solid leads. The primary suspects had all been eliminated as the perpetrators, thus, the case had now entered the cold case status. Sarah however passionately and obsessively followed up on the case, launching her own private investigation, which had also remained fruitless to the present.

Robert Wilson had been eliminated as a suspect, much to Sarah's disappointment as her instincts told her deep down that there was something way off balance about the man. Robert had what seemed like a rock solid alibi though; he had been in a meeting with a Japanese entrepreneur who was remodeling the local mall he had recently acquired. She had overturned every stone and could find no previous relationship with the Oriental man and no reason for that man to have lied for him. Therefore, the captain had eliminated him as a suspect but in Sarah's mind, she knew he had something to do with the kidnapping.

Tyler Howell also sat solemnly at his desk across the office from Sarah. Her partner now for eleven years Tyler thought much like Sarah did, believing that Robert had something to do with the incident involving Angel. His mind refused to stay on the case at hand, that of a forty seven year old discovered by hunters in Center County. It was more than likely a hunting accident, but the case given to him by the boss for a final review, before he closed it for good.

The man was dressed in camouflage with a bright orange vest and hat. More than likely a hunting accident had been the cause of a severed femoral artery that had taken the middle-aged hunters life. As soon as the autopsy was in, he would sign off on it if all were as he suspected. His thoughts wandered back to a case he had not yet solved that of a beautiful little girl of seven. Angel occupied his thoughts almost daily during the past four weeks since her vanishing, as did the girl's mother with her anguished eyes and sad face. A fist came out of nowhere and struck the pile of folders on his desk.

"I know the bastard did it," he hissed under his breath. The thought invoked such fury in him he had to take a deep breath and exhale slowly while counting to ten. He utilized the anger management that all officers were required to learn. He had nearly gone out of his mind years earlier as a rookie investigator solving the crimes of undeserving death and the human monsters that committed them.

Tyler's fist had reacted quicker than his brain as the face of Robert Wilson had flashed through his mind along with that of Rebecca's beautiful battered face. He had observed the bruises while questioning her and as her tears fell, they liquefied the makeup with which she had attempted to cover them. Fighting to keep control of the hate that surged through him, he recalled the fear he had seen in that pretty woman's face and the anguish in her eyes at losing her child. In addition, deep inside he knew that Robert had something to do with the child too. He just had not been able to prove it.

"Rebecca" he sighed to himself, I promised one day to solve this case and I swear to you I will. I'll drag that son-of-a-bitch in for what he did to that little girl and to you! Better yet I should just put a bullet in his head" he mussed silently.

Tyler looked across the small room that was he and his partner's office, observed the morose look on Sarah's face, and instinctively knew where her thoughts were also. She had become as readable as a book to him over the years they had worked together. The longer they were together the better he understood and knew her, and secretly, the more he loved her. He kept his feelings tucked safely away for fear it would ruin the bond of friendship they already shared. Little did he know Sarah felt the same, for if he knew of her feelings then surely the fireworks between them would have ignited long ago?

Tyler dated casually and his latest was a real looker, as he was a very handsome man. She was exactly the opposite of Sarah who was short, cute, and motherly. In spite of her girl next-door appearance though she sparked desires in him that no other woman ever had. He was a little afraid of that sexual explosion that he knew she could ignite in him with just the right touch. Therefore, he kept his feelings locked safely away in his heart, padlocked by logic and reasons, the safest lock that ever existed.

Sarah observed Tyler's distant look and knew he was thinking of Angel. She saw the anger seething beneath his calm and quiet demeanor. She had seen him strike the folders, which contained Angel's case and knew the frustration he felt. As she watched him, her secret feelings began to surface again and she squelched them immediately, reminding herself that Tyler was way out of her league. His latest girlfriend was a number ten all the way and she felt grossly inept at about a two, or at least she thought so.

The deep friendship they had developed was of far more importance than her romantic fantasies and bedtime desires. The work they accomplished together was phenomenally the best in the department and she could not overlook that fact either. Both investigators went back to work, shelving the desires and emotions they had just mutually considered revealing. Thus, time would march on and the soul mates meant to be together would be held back by society's logic and reason. The emotions would continue to simmer beneath the surface like a volcano until their resolve cracked and love flowed like lava, consuming everything in its pathway.

CHAPTER 7

Rebecca paced back and forth across the bedroom floor waiting for Robert to return home. He had been gone more than usual in the month since Angel's disappearance. She chalked it up to him not wanting to deal with her constant depression and moodiness of late. She longed for his arms to hold her but at the same moment she knew she would be repulsed by his touch. What had once driven her to the height of desire now sickened her to her stomach.

The first seven months he had been the ultimate lover, taking Rebecca to unbelievable heights of passion and release. He demanded multiple orgasms that she had never believed possible and she had lovingly fulfilled his every whim. Lately though the sex seemed to be all one sided, she had not had an orgasm in months during their bouts of "lovemaking" if you could even call it that anymore. Ninety percent of the time, it was her sucking him off while he painfully grasped her breasts, the other ten percent of the time he fucked her as if she was a hooker or tramp, talking to her as such while he performed his sexual fantasies.

On one occasion, he was drunk and had sodomized her endlessly to the point where she could not sit comfortably for almost a week. That had been the worst yet. He had raped her, taking her repeatedly in spite of her desperate cries for him to stop. She felt dirty and used, cheap and disgusting after that night. She believed he had done it because she had refused to suck him off that night due to her being sore from a beating the night before. After he had methodically sodomized her for hours, getting off numerous times as he plunged his large hard cock into her virginal anus, stopping only when the blood began to run down her thighs.

Robert was disgusted with her of late. She had become weak even in their lovemaking. She allowed him to dominate her now where before she had frequently pursued him sexually, riding him and sucking his balls and cock with abandon. She used to look him in the eyes as they climaxed and when he came deep in her throat. That used to drive him crazy, now she had a faraway look in her eyes as they made love, looking at the ceiling or walls and he knew she was somewhere else.

"Weak fucking bitch" he thought to himself as he sat at his desk at work.

"Too weak to even adventure in the fucking bedroom" he swore under his breath as he slammed his desk drawer shut. Hate filled his soul for her and her sweet cowardly spineless ways. "Why do men want weak women?" he mussed to himself. "Why do so many settle down with sweet motherly souls who are nothing but weak spineless grown up little girls? I want a tough bitch with me who will match wits with me intellectually and physically, not one who simpers and whimpers and whines at the drop of a hat." Robert pulled out a notebook and began to jot his thoughts down for later perusal. On paper, he poured out his hatred, frustration, loathing, and disgust for his woman.

Eventually, his mind turned to Rebecca's little girl and he smiled strangely, suddenly transported to the little cabin in the woods where she waited for him. She waited quietly, now without crying and screaming, stronger already due to his "lessons" in strength. She would become his woman in the next five to seven years. By the time her blood flowed between her legs, she would become a woman as tough as he would, then, only then, he would make her own woman. She would willingly give herself to him. It was difficult to control his desire for her, for her young innocent untouched body, but he was strong he reminded himself. Stronger than the urges of his cock and the desire in his soul to own and consume her. In time, she would come to him and would demand his sexual prowess, his ultimate godlike ownership of her body and soul. Pure strength would drive her, binding them together forever.

CHAPTER 8

Angel sat quietly in the cage, mind drifting to a better time and place, which she had burned into her memory. Her mother's face intruded into the memory, the picture burned forever in her soul. She would never forget her, no matter how much Robert tried to drive it from her mind. One day she vowed she would be free, go back to her momma, and tell her what a terrible man Robert was. Angel worried about her mother too.

"Was Robert hurting her mother too? I will never forget you mommy!" the little girl vowed to herself in the ramshackle dimly lit cabin. Only the mice responded to her voice, rustling shortly it their nests, and then the deadly silence again.

The silence bothered her most, when she thought she could not take it; she would concentrate on her moms face. Maybe if she wished hard enough her mommy would hear her cries for help. Nevertheless, the days carried on and no help came for her, so she built a wall between herself and the terrible man who used to be her step dad. She, her mother, and her deceased father were on one side of the wall and the bad man was on the other.

Even though her father was gone, she felt his presence beside her. He was in heaven now because the cancer bug had taken him away a long time ago. It had actually been only fifteen months, but to Angel it was a lifetime ago. Now the bad man was in their life and she begged her daddy to come and take them away. How

28

she wished he had not died because they would still be with him and the bad man would never have been in their lives. Thus, Angel built her walls and steeled herself against the one who had hurt them and destroyed their lives.

"I will get away one day and find my mom," she vowed aloud to the dim light heard only by sleeping rodents. And at that moment the seed of strength was planted in her soul and would grow. Nevertheless, would it be soon enough to triumph over the evil that Robert would attempt to plant in her soul, would she triumph over the terrible evil that he planned for her future.

Angel's thoughts were jolted out of their reverie by the sound of tires on gravel and her heart fell. He was back and the lessons would continue. However, she was starving, although she would rather be hungry than endure the painful things he was putting her thru. She steeled her mind against the fear before he entered the door that much she had learned to do already. She pictured her mother and father in her mind and concentrated on them as she endured his "lessons."

One of Robert's favorites was to strap her to cold metal table and stick her with various sized needles. There were tiny red marks all over her tender young body, some of them now inflamed and infected. Her tender feminine spots hurt her the most. Angel had not bathed since she was confined to the awful place, so not only were the marks infected but she itched all over too. Lice crawled in her hair and at night, the roaches scoured her body for food. She had eaten nothing but eggs and dry toast for the last seven months, even that was only every couple of days. Her petite little body had begun to show serious signs of malnutrition and her ribs now showed through her chest muscles.

Robert entered the cabin quietly and looked it over closely. No one had been there as his little booby traps were all still in place. He would know if a spirit had floated through his cabin with all the traps he had set. The seals above the door had been unbroken as were the ones on the two dirty windows. The net over his journals was also perfectly straight and he breathed a sigh of relief. Those damn investigators were hounding him daily and it took a lot of doing to shake them from his tail. He had bought a second vehicle to sneak out of the gym in to remain hidden from their prying eyes.

Angel watched him under lowered lashes pretending to be asleep. Robert had a grocery bag in his hands this time piled high with groceries. Her stomach rumbled involuntarily at the sight of the food. He put the bag on the table and emptied its contents. There were steaks, oranges, vegetables, oatmeal, bacon eggs, milk, peanut butter, jelly, butter, and a loaf of bread. There was even a box of cookies mixed in the other items. The little girl lay there feigning sleep but she did not fool him. Robert smelled her fear.

"Ah, my little Angel, you grow strong already. With you I will succeed in my life's work," he spoke wistfully. A wave of adrenaline washed over him at the thought of her being his, strong and solid.

"It's only been seven months and already you have learned to battle your desires and control your emotions. One day you will give yourself to me wholly and with boldness, strength, and the ultimate of desires. You will love me completely and unconditionally because we will be the same. We will think and act as one and the same" he finished as he cranked up the gas stove.

Angel lay there listening and loathing him. She hated him with every fiber of her young body. She would never even understand completely what he was talking about, but she knew that she would never give him what he wanted.

"Please mom, dad, help me" she cried silently. "Please get me out of here and away from this man!" However, for the time being her fervent prayers would go unanswered.

Robert unlocked her cage and she got up and followed him to the table. She sat in the hard, rickety wooden chair with her back straight, shoulders back and head up. It was the position he liked her to use and it gave her great pride to know that she had beaten the whining and crying that he hated with a passion.

The nearly eight-year-old girl sat like a proud young woman as she awaited her plate of food, and when it finally came, her eyes flickered with disbelief. Her pretty face showed no inkling of emotion; nonetheless, she was awed at the sight of steak, baked potato, fresh hunks of bread spread liberally with butter, and fresh frozen sweet peas. Waiting until he nodded her way, she slowly ate the wonderful repast he had presented her with, savoring every bite.

When she finished eating, she used the toilet, emptied and washed her chamber basin, and then dutifully went to the lesson chair, as she was accustomed to doing. She sat there with a look of hatred and the ever-observant Robert saw it and smiled. He had something different in mind for his little angel today. Trust in her allowed him to return to his truck and retrieve a small box. Returning, he placed it on the floor in front of her.

"The time has come to train your young mind" Robert addressed her. "Open it!"

Angel did so with great trepidation, but kept her fear and anticipation at bay behind a rock solid face. In the box were books. Not the small library books she was accustomed to, but thick books with strange titles. In addition, there were writing workbooks, geography, spelling, Latin, and a mathematics workbook. Over the next six months in captivity little Angel turned eight, learned reading, writing, and arithmetic, and learned all about hate. She read the books, consumed them during the long hours in her cage. Inside, however, the little girl was not daunted, she vowed daily to escape some day and find her way back to the ones she loved. Gripped by her memories of her mother and friends, she focused daily on those loving faces in her soul. She used their visages to keep at bay the hate that attempted to consume her, as it had Adolph Hitler and Robert Wilson.

CHAPTER 9

Rebecca lay in bed dozing lightly, waiting for Robert to come home. She stiffened instinctively when he arrived knowing what was more than likely to come. When he was out late like this, he usually expected her to meet his deviant requests of late. She now loathed that part of their relationship. She lived with it anyway. Angel had disappeared six months earlier, so it mattered little what he did to her body anymore. Her life had ended the moment her little girl had vanished. She stiffened in a natural .reaction to prepare her body for the violent plundering it was about to experience.

Robert opened the bedroom door and watched her lying there, avoiding looking at his face, and he hated her. He smelled her fear and loathed her weakness. However, until his little angel was ready to take him, he had need of Rebecca for his fantasies and sexual release. He had just left his little Angel and it was the reason that his desires were at their greatest peak. He took Rebecca up the ass and then forced her to suck her own excrement from his penis. As he came in her mouth, he looked down at her and hated her, loathed the weak spineless bitch on her knees before him. Angel would-demand one day that he love her like this, she would ride him like a wild mare until she came all over his hard throbbing manhood. Then she would suck his cock and balls, willingly, and with wild abandon. Therefore, he took Rebecca while he fantasized about her daughter. He rode her anus hard

32

and then ejaculated deep in her throat. All the while pretending it was a different time and a different woman. For one day he vowed, Angel would be his, the ultimate of all women.

The next day Rebecca packed a suitcase and left him forever. She checked into a local women's shelter and totally disappeared from Robert s life. She had had her fill of his abuse and sexual deviancy. The shelter took her in and comforted her, supported her; even found her a home to live in. Their counseling program helped her find a good job and eventually she had wiped every aspect of Robert from her life. In the end, she proved stronger than Robert ever imagined and for that reason, he lost her forever. Robert came home late that night and found her gone. The house quiet and empty, but he took it with little anger. Oh, he had to kill her, that much was certain.

He had to crush the life out of her with his bare hands to rid the world of her disgusting weakness. He wanted to choke the life out of her slowly and the very image made him horny so he jerked himself off while watching weak useless whores suck cock on the adult programming station. He fell asleep dreaming of his Angel in the woods and the incredible woman he was going to help her become.

The next morning Robert awoke in a bad mood. With in seconds the events of the night before came flooding back. Rebecca was gone, but he would find her, of that he was certain. Picking up the phone, he dialed the number of a private eye who owed him a few favors. Giving him her information and his cell phone number, he set in motion the wheels of discovery, not that they would yield any answers, but it gave Robert a sense of control over the situation.

Robert then removed every piece of clothing and every photo of her from his home. Lighting a fire in the backyard he burned every remnant of her. He needed no physical property to remember her because his fondest memory would be that of slowly choking the life from the cunt. Finishing his task, he showered and dressed for work, going on with his life as if nothing had happened. This was the way he had trained himself to be, the epitome of strength, the role model for every other human being out there. No bitch was ever going to bring him down, not ever, and those that embarrassed him and shamed him would die the death of the damned that they deserved.

CHAPTER 10

Sarah's passion for the case died slowly, regretfully. No new leads had surfaced and her investigation of Robert had yielded no grounds for an arrest. She sat on her couch, thought about Rebecca, now childless, and wondered how she was doing. She picked up the phone and dialed her number.

"Hello" a male voice answered.

"Is Rebecca there?" Sarah queried.

"No, the bitch left and I'm glad, so don't call back here!" a voice she assumed was Robert's, replied gruffly.

Sarah smiled to herself. "So she finally got the balls to leave him," she thought. I wonder where she is she thought as she picked up the phone to dial Tyler's number.

"Hello?" he answered sending chills up and down her spine at the sound of his husky male voice. Amazing the affect he had on her, but it was one that she would have to keep to herself she mussed regretfully.

"Hi" Sarah replied, sending an equally intense chill down his spine, goose bumps prickling his skin and sending his heart to thumping again. "What's going on?"

"Well, I just found out that Rebecca left Robert. Maybe now we can find her and get something concrete out of her.

"Good thinking, any idea where she is though?"

"Shelters the only place I can readily come up with partner. She had no family and Robert drove away all her friends. She also had very little money or resources. I'll start checking them out tomorrow" Sarah finished.

"Sounds like a plan! By the way, how are you and the kids?" Tyler queried.

"Oh as well as can be expected from a seventeen year old going on thirty."

Tyler chuckled, "I remember all too well when Ashley was seventeen and I don't envy you."

Secretly though, he did. He had wanted another child and he longed to step in where the girl's dead-beat father had fallen way short. Nevertheless, it was not to be so he cut the call short and excused himself with a lie of being tired. Someday, he thought, maybe fate would look his way and grant him his greatest desire. He had even quit taking sexual partners, taking care of his needs the old-fashioned way, all the while thinking of her, his Sarah. As he climbed into bed a few minutes later, his cock was half hard already just thinking of her and the anticipation of his fantasies.

Across town, Sarah was facing the same dilemma, her body running away with her fantasies as she felt involuntary moisture between her legs. As they pleasured themselves, their thoughts merged as one and they rose to the heavenly release as one on the wings of their orgasm.

In a house halfway between them, Robert was fucking a cheap hooker by the name of Kitty, whom he had picked up on Michal an Avenue. He thought of Angel as he sank his cock into her flaccid anus that refused to excite him. His fantasies excited him however, and his cock responded valiantly as he came deep in the woman's bowel. All the while he was thinking of his "woman to be" in the cabin in the hills. A woman that would morph from the child he held captive in his laboratory.

Fair-haired blue-eyed Angel lay in her cage reading the book Robert had left her. She was still oblivious to the desires of puberty so she lay quietly reading the book about supremacy. She could not decipher all the words yet but she figured out enough to know it was another of Roberts hate books. Blacks were called niggers, Italians wops, and Mexicans spics. She drank in the knowledge and filled her head with it but beneath it all, she held on to the teachings of her mother and father; and that was that people were people and all loved by God. She was also beginning to learn the depths of Robert's hatred for people that were different, she did not understand it, but she knew of its existence.

Rebecca went on with her life, saddened by her lost relationship, but with a relief and complete freedom, she had nearly forgotten even existed. She landed a good job at a local hospital in Philadelphia as a surgical RN and soon purchased her own home. She kept to herself and did not date due to the sour taste she still had in her mouth from Robert and his psychosis.

It would be many months would brave a date and it would take a very special man to entice her to do so. Deep inside she continued to grieve for her lost child and never gave up hope that she was somewhere alive and thinking of her. Rebecca remembered her Angel every day and voiced a heavenward prayer for her little girl. She prayed for God to give her little girl a guardian angel to see her through protect her and comfort her. Little did she know, Angel's guardian angel was already there, sitting in the rafters of the hunting shack ready to step in should the need arise when the girl's life was in danger.

The angel overhead kept fresh in the little girls mind the love and memories of her dear mother and heaven sent father. He would make her the woman she would become and give her strength against the evil forces that were alive and thriving in Robert. A terrible evil that he was determined to plant and grow in the little girl he had kidnapped.

CHAPTER 11

Sarah and Tyler sat across from each other at her desk in the small office they shared. It was the one-year anniversary of Angel's disappearance. They each scoured over the files page by page to ascertain whether they had missed something. Sarah's interview with Rebecca had produced nothing concrete concerning the case. It had merely solidified what they had already suspected about the abuse she had suffered at Robert's hand. Unfortunately, that did not make him a kidnapper or murderer.

Surveillance on Robert had yielded nothing either. He worked, went to the local gym faithfully, and went to his little hunting cabin in the mountains occasionally. Now and then, he picked up local hookers, but interviews with them only yielded a slightly deviant sexual appetite. They even knew about the second vehicle that he had purchased and drove in an attempt to throw them off his tail. They still had no grounds to yank him in and interrogate him. However, both parties felt that a major piece of the puzzle was missing. One little tip would turn the tables and crack the case wide open, if only they could discover it before it was too late and the girl was discovered dead. For hours, they reviewed the files before giving up once more.

"Want to get a bite to eat?" Tyler asked, sighing deeply. "I think we need to take a break."

"Sure" Sarah said with a sigh. "We aren't getting anywhere here anyway except driving ourselves crazy!"

"Tell me about it! I know he's involved somehow though, somehow, some way he had that child kidnapped."

"I know Tyler, but we have to prove if and that seems to be impossible" she replied sympathetically.

"But I will prove it if it's the last thing I do!" Tyler responded vehemently.

"I know" Sarah replied with conviction. "It is a promise we made to Rebecca a year ago, and I intend to keep it!"

"So where do we get a bite to eat?"

"Your pick" Sarah replied with a smile.

"I'll surprise you" he spoke to her gently, the emotions beginning to stir in his heart, and he won temporarily.

Dinner was at a quiet little Japanese steakhouse downtown. It had a quiet soothing atmosphere but not too elegant. It was perfect, their kind of place. They ordered and talked small talk as they awaited their plates of food. After the food arrived, they ate quietly, each lost in their own private thoughts, invoked by the candlelight and romantic atmosphere. Once he caught her eye and he nearly choked on the piece of meat he was chewing as he saw the raw emotion raging in her eyes. He looked away but not quickly enough as her gray eyes mirrored her soul for just a moment and he knew she felt for him exactly the way he felt or her.

"How long?" he wondered to himself had she been hiding her feelings from him.

Excitement sent a chill down his spine, anticipation of her soft willing lips sweet beneath his. He would take her to the park and walk with her, letting the pent up emotions slowly surface. It was time, way past time when they should have been exposed. Whatever the future held was uncertain, but he was sure this night would change their lives forever. As long as Sarah felt for him the way he did for her, and from what he had just seen in her eyes that she did, it would be a wonderful future.

"Let's go to the park," he said abruptly, trying to catch her eye again, but they were lowed demurely. Glancing away, she flushed bright red and swallowed hard. Tyler smiled, tenderness playing in his eyes, his face relaxed to ease her discomfort. He suddenly realized that she had been fighting the feelings just as he had, and probably for some time now.

"Tyler,' she said softly, "is this really a good idea?"

"Yes, it's the best idea I've had in a long time" he whispered. "It's way past time for this rendezvous to happen!"

Sarah blushed, emotions welling up within her heart, emotions she had fought for so long to keep inside she was not quite sure how to let them show. She looked up at Tyler's handsome face, his full lips and dark eyes and she saw the love pouring from his soul and etched on his face. The thrill she felt was nearly unbearable and her hands shook as she grabbed her purse and jacket.

"Let me" he said, taking her jacket and helping her put it on.

"Thanks" she returned," always the perfect gentleman."

"I may not be the perfect gentleman tonight, you may change your mind about that!" he replied chuckling.

"Never" she smiled back, shivering as his fingers brushed her collarbone, her panties suddenly wet with her pent up desires.

Tyler felt his cock begin to grow and was thankful he already had his jacket on to hide the proof of his desire for her. Taking her hand, he led her to his Durango and helped her in. Getting into the drivers seat he slid the key into the ignition and instead of cranking the engine, he laid his hand on her thigh and gently caressed her face with the other. Leaning in he kissed her, softly playing with her lips with his until he heard her moan of pleasure. At that moment, he slid his tongue into her sweet mouth and explored the hot wet crevices. She tasted better than he had ever imagined and he felt her chest arch with desire to have his hands on her breasts.

More than willing he fondled her, firmly and slowly grasping a nipple between his thumb and forefinger and listened to her gasps of pleasure the act elicited from her. Hesitantly, she touched him, his face, his chest, and then his hard huge cock. She heard his sharp intake of breath when she touched him there and smiled to herself. It was all she had imagined, all she had dreamed of, desired, wanted, and loved. Tyler felt the same as he pulled reluctantly away from her, started the SUV and started for the park.

Arriving at their destination, Tyler went around the vehicle and helped her down from her seat. He could not get over his luck, his fortune; he never believed she felt for him as he did her. Not in a million years could he have imagined that she loved him as much as he loved her. He held her to his body for a moment to be sure he was not dreaming. The firm pressures of her body against his assured him that he was not in dreamland and he clasped her to him reveling in the feel of her against him. Soft and willing yet firm and demanding with all her two years of pent up emotions.

Grasping her hand, he led her to the trees, the late summer breeze caressing their faces. He kissed her gently at first and then with more and more passion and desire. His hard cock pressed against her thigh as she kneaded against him, needing him, wanting him. Before they knew it, they were naked in the starlight, the moonlight glistening on their sweating and heaving bodies. Tyler drank in her body, beautiful in the moonlight. Her breasts were taut and full, her hips rounded sensuously and her stomach taut and her stomach flat and tight. Her crop of closely manicured hair at the V of her legs beckoned him and when he touched her there, she melted against him moaning her pleasure. She grasped his hard well-endowed cock and stroked him slowly and he felt his knees turn to jelly and his head began to spin.

Taking her with him, he knelt to the ground and knelt between her trembling legs. He took her slowly, filling her completely in the hot wet secret place that he had been longing for. Hugging his manhood with her inner muscles, she matched him thrust for thrust until they reached ecstasy as one.

CHAPTER 12

Rebecca sat in the cafeteria of the hospital she worked at, eating a salad and chicken wrap for lunch. A male voice suddenly interrupted her thoughts.

"Is this seat taken?" asked a handsome young man in his late thirties to early forties.

"No" she replied shyly.

"May I sit here?" he asked gently noticing the deer in the headlights look in her eyes.

"I gu-guess" she stammered back.

"I'm Byron Welty" he introduced himself as he took the vacant seat next to her.

"Who is the beautiful lady I have the pleasure of meeting today?"

"Rebecca" she replied succinctly.

They ate together in silence and when they had nearly finished he handed her his business card.

"If you'd like to get out one evening give me a ring, no strings attached, just friends.

Rebecca nodded and taking the card, she dropped it in her uniform pocket. She would toss it later when he was gone she told herself. He was tall, good-looking, sexy, any girls dream date, which was exactly why she wanted to close the door and lock it before she even became interested in him. Her heart was not yet ready to take a chance on love so putting him out of her mind,

42

she went back to work and soon forgot the encounter.

Almost a week later, she was getting her uniforms together to wash them when she came across the card. She could still see his dancing hazel eyes and perfect smile. His lithe body with its broad shoulders and narrow hips, flat stomach and nicely rounded backside. Shaking her head, she threw the card in the trashcan next to the washer. She was never again going to allow herself to fall for partner's looks and charm. She had allowed it to happen with Robert and had lived to regret it, had been devastated by her love for him. Going on with her chores she soon forgot the tall handsome stranger again.

That night she tried to sleep but sleep eluded her. She kept seeing Byron's handsome face every time she closed her eyes. His dancing eyes and perfect smile haunted her. After tossing and turning for a while, she finally got up and retrieved his card from the trashcan. Staring at the card for a few minutes, she finally gave in to her instinct and dialed the number.

"Hello" answered a deep male voice.

"Hello" she answered back timidly, "this is Rebecca, and we met at the hospital.

"Why hello there, I was beginning to think you'd thrown my number away.

"Well actually I did yesterday but tonight I couldn't sleep and thought maybe talking with a friend might help.

"You mean you dug in the trash to get my number. Now that is something of a first. No woman I've ever dated could even top that one."

"It wasn't at all like that" she replied blushing a deep red, thankful he could not see her face just then.

"So how is life treating you?" he asked to break the tension.

"Fine" she replied, still hesitant to take the road her heart was tempted to. His husky voice tugged at her though and made her want to get to know him better. They started out with small talk and before she knew it, they had talked for over an hour. She had agreed to go to a movie that they both wanted to see, but she made it plain there were no strings attached.

She could not get over how easily they had clicked and how compatible they seemed for each other. However, he did not know a lot about her yet and would probably never speak to her again after she divulged all her mistakes, misery, and woes. Tears pricked her eyes as she recalled the degradation and humiliation she had suffered at Roberts hands. In her heart, she had vowed no man would ever do that to her again, including the handsome truck driver, Byron David Welty.

PART 2

HOPE AND REVERANCE

CHAPTER 13

Sunlight filtered through a dirty window and gently caressed the sleeping child curled in a tattered blanket. Tweeting birds and sparkling dew on the grass outside the cabin mingled with the warm rays of sunlight to herald the fresh arrival of spring. Slowly, Angel sketched her lithe young body bathed in the warm rays that turned her dirty blond hair into a golden mass around her head.

Size four feet touched cold metal snapping Angel out of her dreamy sleep into full awareness of her predicament. Big wide eyes perused the cage and the cabin beyond. No one had arrived to rescue her and she was definitely not caught in some atrocious nightmare. For that matter, no one had arrived to torture her either. Robert had been gone for two days again and Angel knew by experience now that he would arrive some time today.

Her stomach rumbled with hunger as the small amount of food he left her each time had been finished the night before. The odor of feces and urine wafting from the basin in the corner of her prison reminded her too that he was due to arrive any time now. She had exhausted the stack of books he would left and she was eager for him to replace them with fresh material. Angel literally devoured the books mentally. The last one she would read was "Of Mice and Men", a sad tale of a boy a boy who was rather dumb from birth. He had gone and unwittingly killed a woman and then was killed by his brother before the men could capture and punish him. There were times she wished she would just die or that Robert would kill her, especially when looking into the future at her life in the dog cage and Roberts's lessons of torture.

Lately, Robert had been tempering tender moments with painful lessons. On good days, he would talk with her of their future, spinning fantasies of the two of them taking the world by storm and making their legacy together. She could imagine little of what he was saying and spun fantasies of her own to his animated voice. One day she would be free of him and would find her momma. Patiently she waited, biding her time until the moment arrived when she would escape from him forever.

Several hours later, her thoughts were broken by the sound of gravel crunching under the tires of Robert s truck. The girl sat up and positioned her body in the standard Indian style of sitting. Within seconds, the scared girl morphed into a young woman child, masking her true emotions with those of anticipation, appreciation, toughness and attitude. It was the look, which she had learned pleased him the most. The door swung open and he stood there, shortly perusing the cabin to be sure all his security devices were still in place. Satisfied, his gaze finally rested on the young woman-child in the cage at the center of the cabin. He read the anticipation on her face mingled with gratefulness for his company, but he also saw the set jaw and little bits of anger glinting in her eyes as well. His face broke into a wide appraising grin; his little Angel was slowly becoming his woman.

Turning he walked out the door and returned moments later, arms laden with grocery bags. A second trip produced a cardboard box of books, paper, pencils and various other learning materials. A third trip produced a small pet carrier and a bag of items in a Wal Mart bag. Angel's excitement grew but she kept it in check, remaining motionless while Robert put food away and retrieved pots and pans from the dish drainer. The cooking utensils gleamed now unlike the dirty ones he had used months before, thanks to Angel's cleaning them after each use.

"Today I'm going to teach you how to make fried chicken and French fries" he informed her while unlocking the cage door.

"Yes sir" the woman child acknowledged with respect as her stomach rumbled and her mouth watered. Robert took her hand and helped her from the cage taking her momentarily into his arms and hugging her. She relaxed immediately as she had programmed herself to react when he showed her affection, pretending she liked it. Actually, she did like it until she remembered the other side of the man and she had to fight the fear and loathing that welled up inside her like bile from her stomach.

For the next hour or so, she carefully followed Roberts's directions. Still amazed that she had done it to perfection, she sat down with him to enjoy the scrumptious meal of fried chicken, French fries and salad. She savored every bite, chewing thoroughly and following the rules of etiquette that had been taught her by her captor. Robert watched her with open appraisal and self-acknowledgement at how far she had come and how quickly she had learned from him. Seven months had turned the sniveling little brat that he had known into a smarter, tougher, and more mature little woman child. She would continue, he hoped, to develop into a strong, intelligent, spitfire of a woman, both strong and of superior intelligence, as he was.

After cleaning up dinner, he instructed Angel to put water on to heat for a bath. She hurried to do his bidding, grateful for the chance to wash her itchy skin and hair. After dumping the water into a large Rubbermaid tub, she shed her panties, oversized t-shirt, and climbed in under Roberts's watchful eye. It was another of the uncomfortable actions she had learned to live with in order to acquire the necessities of life. As she climbed in, he brought her a gift bag and instructed her to open it.

Angel opened the bag with quiet eagerness, delight shimmering in her eyes but held in check so as not to anger her captor. Robert hated overly exhibited emotions of delight,

anticipation, sorrow, eagerness, and affection. On the other
hand, he attempted to draw out of her such emotions as anger,
ambivalence, desire, aggression, and even hatred. Inside the bag,
she discovered a soft green bath sponge, body wash, shampoo,
lotion, and a comb.

"It's time you start to smell like a young lady instead of a
polecat!" Robert exclaimed gruffly, masking the desire he felt for
her soft youthful body. In time, she would bud and blossom,
but for now he would have to be satisfied with the occasional
glimpses of her body that he stored in his memory and retrieved
later on to use when he was with his whores.

Angel bathed slowly, savoring the feel of the sponge and the
wonderful scent of the body wash. Scrubbing her hair with real
shampoo instead of bar soap was sheer heaven and she finally
climbed out of the tub half an hour later, pink and gleaming.
Robert threw her a new pink fluffy towel that was incredibly soft
and wrapped all the way around her body twice.

"Come here little lady" Robert said softly, "I have some more
surprises for my little lady!" She went to him, her little heart
hammering deep in her chest, her eyes lowered respectfully to
mask the fear mirrored there.

"Today is a special day for us," he said slowly. "We reach a
new level of trust and communication today. You are my little
woman and it is time you begin to dress and act the part. I have
brought you new clothes, hygiene products, bedclothes, and a
very, very special gift which you will receive later."

"Yes sir" Angel replied with respect and humility.

"Angel" he said softly, almost tenderly. "Look at me." She
complied.

"You will address me as Robert from here on out. I am
your mentor. I am your teacher, but I am also your friend and
companion. You are my little lady and it is time you begin to
address me as such and call me Robert."

"Yes Robert" she said softly but still with feigned respect.

Inside she still hated him but now she began to feel very confused as Robert began to play a new game. A game he played would attempt to win the now toughened little girl over to him. He would play on her emotions and her needs while still asserting himself as her teacher and mentor. He handed her another bag, which contained several pairs of denim shorts in various colors, pretty shirts, and a six pack each of socks and frilly lace panties. Tears shimmered in her eyes as she gratefully accepted the articles and dressed slowly in an outfit he had picked out for her. Completing the outfit, he handed her a pair of shiny white sandals. For the first time in seven months, Angel looked at Robert with real affection and gratitude. In addition, this was just the beginning of his seduction of the woman child. The game was afoot and he was more determined than ever to win.

An hour later Angel stood before him shoulders back and head held high. Her long blonde hair fastened with a ponytail holder hung softly down her back in natural, ringlets. Her face was one of promising beauty with her small nose, large brown eyes, high cheekbones, and soft full lips.

Robert looked her over from head to toe and was immensely pleased with his creation thus far.

The proud stance she took with her head held high but her chin tucked in observance of his dominion over her. She was the perfect woman in his mind, but one that was still in the body of a child. He would have the delightful honor of watching her grow and develop and Robert felt the stirring of desire in his loin, so he changed his line of thought quickly. For the next few hours, he had her read to him aloud from a book on the evolution of the KKK. He made her stand straight, holding the book up and speaking loudly and clearly. When she stumbled over a word her corrected her and had her repeat the word five times, so she would remember it next time. Thus, he balanced his affection with discipline and in his mind; he was creating the perfect mate for himself.

CHAPTER 14

Saturday morning found Rebecca sitting at her breakfast nook drinking coffee and reading the morning paper. The paper was a habit she had added to her daily routine after the disappearance of her daughter. She would read each page front to back hoping for some article that might clue her in to what had happened to her daughter. She paid special attention to the police blotter and obituaries searching for clues or a case similar to hers.

At lunchtime, she gave up the search and went to shower. As she undressed she perused her body in the mirror from her pretty face with the large dark blue eyes to her small but pert breasts, flat stomach, slightly protruding hipbones, still firm softly rounded bottom, and long slender legs. She was in bad need of a tan but otherwise she agreed with the mirror that she was not a bad looking woman for forty. Her bosom and bottom had just the slightest droop thanks to her daily walking routine.

Rebecca's mind wandered to Byron and apprehension began to build.

"Would he like her body? Would he throw her away after discovering the trauma she'd suffered at Robert s hands" the questions raced through her mind as she prepared for the evening out. Turning her hair irons on she sighed and stepped into the shower. She let the hot water wash over her for several minutes relaxing the tension caused by her straying mind.

Dressed in Levis and a snug button down blouse she took one last glance in the mirror. She took in her deep dark blue eyes and slim figure, the top of her breasts just slightly peeking out the top of her blouse. She decided then that at forty she was still a knockout. Confidence returned and she headed for the kitchen to find the phone book and schedule some tanning sessions. She also made an appointment at the salon to her hair and nails done.

Grabbing her purse, she set out to begin her long day of pampering herself, one well deserved after the months she had spent at home not caring one way or another how she looked. Rebecca returned home at six p.m. after treating herself to a chicken wrap from Wendy's and several new outfits from the local mall. Anticipation was building and so was her apprehension. It was quickly approaching seven p.m. when Byron was to pick her up and the butterflies had already begun.

Part of her mind was anticipating with excitement the evening out with a handsome man and the rest of her mind faced it with trepidation due to her experience with Robert. Determined to enjoy herself she shut Robert out of her mind, after all, this was simply a no strings attached outing to the movies as friends. Putting on a Johnny Cash CD, she sat at the kitchen table and waited for the minutes to tick on by until Byron knocked on her front door.

CHAPTER 15

Across town, Sarah sat at her kitchen table after she had had dinner with her youngest daughter, Michelle, now seventeen and a striking beauty. They talked about school and the track team competitions Michelle had been to, and her placing in them. She had been close to all her children, even through the many battles of the teen years. Conversing had been one of Sarah's strong points with her children, from way back when they were very young and she had kept the strategy of child rearing based around that focal point. Tonight Tyler and she would break the news to Michelle of their relationship.

Sarah was only slightly apprehensive because for years her daughters had tried to convince Sarah to date and find a companion to complete her life. Tyler was a dear friend however, and Sarah was a little uncertain what her girls' reaction would be to her getting involved with her partner, and their family friend.

"Tyler's coming over in a little while," Sarah said casually to her daughter. "Are you going to be home tonight?"

"Yes mom, I'll be here. I have a test to study for and finals are right around the corner too."

Pride filled Sarah's soul as she took in her daughters' beauty and reflected on her daughter's dedication to school and achieving good grades. She was also number one on her track team, partly due her long slender but muscular legs and in part due to her hard work and dreams of becoming an Olympic contender one day.

"Good, we need to discuss something with you before you get too caught up in you studies" Sarah said light heartedly so as not to give the secret away before it was time.

"What is it mom? Have you decided to marry that hunk of a partner you have or what?" Michelle jested lightly. "I know if he was my partner I'd have snatched him up a long time ago!"

Sarah swallowed hard. "Not so fast little lady, if you girls had your way you would have married me off long ago!"

"Well mom, you're a pretty woman and a good woman, but more than that, you deserve a good man instead of spending every night alone."

"If she only knew" Sarah smiled to herself. "When the right one comes along it will happen," she said to her daughter, nearly blushing as she remembered Tyler's tender kisses the night before. She said nothing more because she wanted Tyler there to break the news, now worried even less about Michelle's reaction after listening to her daughters light bantering. Moments later, the doorbell rang and she let Michelle answer if confident that Tyler would handle everything with tact and grace.

"Where's that good-looking mom of yours?" Tyler's deep voice reverberated through the house. Sarah thought how nice it would be to hear that voice every day when she awoke. Involuntarily her nipples hardened and she became moist just at the thought of his touch each night in her bed.

"I'm right here," Sarah said, forcing her thoughts to the present as she joined Tyler and her daughter in the living room. Tyler sat in the recliner and to Sarah he suddenly looked as if he belonged there, as if the chair was placed there just for him.

"How's school going?" Tyler addressed Michelle.

"Great! Finals are coming up though and track meets are two or three times a week now. I am a very busy person so go ahead and tell me the big news. Did you get fired or get a promotion?" she joked with him.

"No, I've taken on another job though, a very big and very

important job for that matter.

"Really, that's very interesting, but how are you going to find time to see us then? It's hard enough with the hours you work, and you're going to squeeze another job into your schedule!" Michelle exclaimed with a little disappointment in her voice. Tyler had become the male role model in Michelle's life and she adored and idolized him, especially after she realized what a deadbeat her own father was.

"Well I guess I'll just have to marry your mother and move in with you all!" Tyler said softly with mischief dancing in his eyes.

"If she wasn't such a spinster she'd have married you a long time ago!" Sarah's daughter teased back at them.

"What do you think Sarah? Are you going to listen to your daughter and marry me?"

Sarah froze as she saw the look in his eyes. He was not joking by his expression, he was actually proposing to her in front of her daughter. He reached into his sports jacket and retrieved a little gold box. Her heart started to pound as she realized the depth of his question. It was all too much, too sudden, much too sudden. They had only just discovered their feelings for each other.

"Mom, oh mom, you've just got to say yes!" her daughter cried out with elation and excitement at the irony of her teasing and the event unfolding before her very eyes. Sarah's eyes filled with tears, tears of joy and happiness as she gazed in wonder at the sincerity in Tyler's eyes and then at the beautiful gold box lying in his hand.

"Come on Sarah, we've known each other for years now. It is not as if we just met yesterday and jumped right into bed the first night. Besides we aren't getting any younger either," Tyler said huskily. She blushed as she saw her daughter stifle a giggle.

"Come on mom, you've just got to say yes! He'd be the greatest husband and father, I just know he would!" Sarah went to him and knelt between his knees, kissed him softly and then gazed deep into his eyes.

"Yes, I would love the pleasure of having you as my husband" she said with deep emotion, tears shimmering on her cheeks. She liked the sound of the word husband in her ears as her daughter threw her arms around both of them, tears running down her cheeks as well. The excitement was palpable, excitement for the future and the family they would create.

"Bye dad" Michelle said softly. Got to go, my finals won't wait" and she quietly left the two wrapped in each other's arms, reveling in the ecstasy of their coming union.

CHAPTER 16

The sun was just setting when Robert finally relieved Angel of the book in her hands and allowed her a drink of water. As she drank, he retrieved the small canvas pet carrier from the corner where he had placed it. Eager, but the picture of calmness Angel watched as he unzipped the bag reached in and removed a small puppy. Her eyes drank in the sight of the little animal as her heart pounded with hope in her chest.

"Come hear Angel." Robert instructed her. Walking over to him, she could barely hold her excitement in check as she gazed upon the wiggling little puppy he held in his hands.

"I know you get awful lonely up here when I'm not around, so I brought you a little companion."

"Thank-you very much sir" Angel said with gratitude.

"You are to care for him, feed him, water him, and clean up after him. I will provide you with everything you need to do so," Robert instructed with a commanding tone in his voice once more. He must not let her think that he felt anything like kindness or pity that would weaken him in her eyes and give her an opportunity to prey upon his emotions. She must continue her training until she became the perfect woman for him.

He spent the next hour going over his strict rules as to the caring and cleaning up after the little dog. She was to feed him so many pieces of dry dog food from Ziploc bag of Puppy Chow. Plastic bags and newspaper left outside the cage within easy reach along with a gallon jug of water and a small plastic cup and bowl. The box of food had also contained a jar of peanut butter, half a loaf of wheat bread, a pop-off top can of tuna, raviolis, and sardines. A new fleece blanket, fluffy pillow, and pillowcase were in the bottom of the box and Angel accepted each proffered gift gratefully. By eight o-clock, Robert had placed her back in the cage where she made herself comfortable as he placed two new books beside the cage. He placed a plate of chicken and fries, now cold, beside her prison, handed her the puppy, and clicked the padlock back in place.

Tears welled up in Angels eyes as she heard the crunch of gravel beneath the trucks departing wheels, but this time she only cried for a few minutes as the puppy in her arms began whining and licking her tears. She held him for several hours petting him and sharing a chicken leg with him. Angel curled up with her wonderful new companion and began her nightly ritual of remembering her mother and father. She had to concentrate a lot harder now as some of her memories had begun to fade with time, and soon she fell asleep,

CHAPTER 17

Byron woke Sunday morning and the first thing he recalled was the face of the most incredible woman he had ever met. He felt like a teenager with his first steady girlfriend. Humming the whole way through his shower and personal hygiene routine, he was dumbfounded at his good luck. "Perhaps Destiny has finally smiled upon me," he whispered and the mirror reflected a boyish grin on his handsome face.

Standing in front of a full-length mirror in his snug boxers, he looked over his forty two year old body with a critical eye. Broad shoulders tapered to narrow hips and long muscular legs that complimented his six-foot frame. Bright green-gray eyes, high cheekbones, narrow tapered nose, high forehead and a generous sprinkle of freckles bore visual evidence of his Welsh heritage.

"Over all" he thought to himself, "quite a handsome face even with my receding hairline."

He laughed at his egotistical opinion of himself, flashing perfectly aligned, beautiful teeth. Hopefully, Rebecca would have the same opinion and would overlook the fine lines on his face. To boot he had a slight bulge his belly had acquired over the years of being an over the truck driver.

Tonight he would wow her with dinner at his place. His menu began with shrimp cocktail appetizers followed by grilled T-bones, veggie kabobs, baked potatoes, and salad. If his looks did not win her over than surely his cooking skills would. He made a quick list, grabbed his coupons, and headed to the store, pealing out of the driveway in his brand new Dodge Charger. An hour later, he was back home and cleaning his three-bedroom doublewide. Three hours later the four-year-old bachelor pad looked much more presentable for Rebecca to spend the evening in.

Next, he prepared the salad, cleaned, and cut up the veggies for the kabobs. Sweet red peppers, yellow peppers, fresh mushrooms, sweet onions, tiny cherry tomatoes filled small metal skewers. On afterthought, he placed a couple of the giant tiger shrimp between the veggies for a perfect surf and turf appeal. Forty-five minutes later he had the potatoes scrubbed, buttered and wrapped in foil, the steaks rubbed with his own homemade blend of seasonings. Dinner under control, he went to change clothes and spruce up for the arrival of the one who was the reason his heart kept skipping all day.

Across town, Rebecca stepped out of a steaming shower and threw on her light green fleece bathrobe. She ironed the frizz from her long black hair that morphed back to curly at the slightest hint of humidity or moisture. She was thankful the evening forecast was to be warm but slightly breezy, which meant no humidity. She chose a matching set of lingerie, though she had no intention of sleeping with Byron, a woman never could be sure. Snug Levis and a short-sleeved white v-neck blouse enhanced her still pert buttocks and C-cup breasts. At forty, she was still a good-looking woman with only the finest of lines around her eyes. Black cowgirl boots completed her outfit and make-up carefully applied, she headed downstairs. Grabbing the directions from the kitchen table, she carefully locked her doors and headed for Byron's house.

Ten minutes later Rebecca pulled up to the lot where Byron lived. She took in the landscaping, large deck, and newer model mobile home and was impressed. He apparently was responsible and took care of his possessions. It was not a big house such as Robert owned but it was nice. Rebecca was not a woman impressed by money, cars, and big houses, but it did show that Byron was hard working and responsible. He had told her of his marriage failing and how he had walked out with next to nothing and had started over. He had done well for a forty-two year old bachelor.

Just as she opened her car door, Byron walked out onto the deck with a plate of steaks in one hand and a long grilling fork in the other. He waved with the fork hand and smiled, her heart dropped to her stomach. He had a beautiful smile, when he did so, it reached up to his bright green eyes and you knew it was sincere. He was dressed in Levis and an obviously Floridian shirt with palm trees on it. The shades of green in the shirt brought out the green in his eyes and made them mesmerizing to look at. She walked nervously towards him as he lifted the grill lid and placed the steaks on the grill where they sizzled, making her stomach growl quietly.

"Well I see you found me."

"No problem, I can tell you drive for a living because you give very good directions."

"Anytime you need to find your way somewhere just give me a call," Byron said with a deep chuckle. "By the way, how do you like your steak?"

"Medium is fine, a little red in the middle, but no blood."

"Same here, I like my cow to have quit bleeding before I eat it." While Byron cooked they talked, laughed, and soon became very comfortable with each other's company, setting the stage for a beautiful evening.

CHAPTER 18

The bridal march echoed through the old United Methodist church from the pipe organ that consumed the entire front wall of the little church. Sunlight filtered through stained windows creating a kaleidoscope of colors on the white wall of the sanctuary. A sweet perfume of fresh roses mingled with the cool air blowing silently from air ducts in the ceiling. Overhead strip lighting bathed the guests softly, adding to the hushed, expectant atmosphere as the stood peering at the foyer doors. Sarah stood on the other side of that door, her heart hammering and her throat choking back tears of happiness. Her man waited at the altar for her, her dream-guy, her soul mate. They had had a whirlwind romance over the last six months and the friendship they had shared for years had solidified and from it had grown a deep beautiful love.

Tyler stood nervously at the front of the church one hand in his pocket clutching the ring that would symbolize their eternal union. His mind whirled as memories flashed through his mind of the past six months with Sarah. Briefly, thoughts of the coming night with her sent shivers down his spine. They had not shared a bed since he had proposed to her in her living room, and he had to hold his member in check as it threatened to react to his thoughts. Then the door opened, the sight drew his attention back to the moment as his beautiful bride drew an audible gasp from the audience. Slowly she gracefully walked the rose petal laden runner to the altar, where he stood waiting patiently to begin their union. Their eyes locked together the moment the door opened and they never broke their gaze until she turned and handed the matron of honor, her oldest daughter, Annie, her bouquet of roses.

The ceremony went quickly for them both, they said their vows, their prayers, lit a unity candle, and exchanged rings. In no time, at all she was Mrs. Tyler Howell. Tyler bent and she stood on tiptoes and they shared the sweetest kiss they had ever shared. It was a kiss of such devotion, promise, love, commitment, and sexual energy that she began to tremble. He pulled her tighter to his chest sharing with her his physical energy as well. At that very moment, she knew she had found her soul mate, her true love, and her life partner, the one who would fulfill her deepest desires and wildest fantasies.

CHAPTER 19

Nights were still cold up in the mountains of Clinton County and the morning sun warmed the tiny cabin where the little girl and her new puppy lay sleeping. Snuggled together under a new flannel blanket, Angel's pretty head lay on an equally new pillow and as the little girl-child awoke; she was warm and did not ache from sleeping on the hard floor of the cage, as she had grown accustomed to. Her thoughts strayed to Robert and his sudden acts of kindness.

"Why was he being so kind to her after months and endless months of torturous lessons?" She asked herself, still remembering vividly the pins he had stuck her with while she lay upon a cold steel table, her head held in a vice and her wrists and ankles restrained in leather straps. She had learned not to whimper or cry out not to complain or whine. He taught her how to endure incredible pain, to hold her emotions inside, bite her lip and still her quivering muscles. The man who would come to see her yesterday was kinder and gentler than she had ever known him to be, even when her mommy had been with them too. Pulling the puppy closer she laid for a while, grateful for Robert's gifts but puzzled as to his sudden change in behavior. She read the titles of the new books he had brought her trying to decide which one to read first. "Tale of Two Cities" was a hardback and "Catcher in the Rye" was a small paperback.

She chose the small paperback, placed her little puppy on a

piece of newspaper, and waited for him to do his business while she squatted over a small bucket to do hers. Puppy droppings and pee cleaned up she used an alcohol wipe to clean her hands after tying the mess up in a paper bag and placing it outside the cage. She then counted out twenty-five pieces of puppy food and slipped into it some slivers of chicken she had saved him from the night before. After making a peanut butter sandwich she poured each of them a little water and with the puppy resting on her chest, she lay back propped on her new fluffy pillow and began her book.

CHAPTER 20

They made a good-looking couple. He was fair skinned, fair haired, and handsome. Freckles that covered his face, his arms, and his chest, where his shirt was unbuttoned, added to his good looks instead of taking away from them. She was of a darker complexion and her Italian facial features were sharper in contrast to his more rounded ones. They were complete opposites but as they talked and laughed together, they discovered they had much in common. Both had been hurt deeply by the people they loved, they had been cheated on and abused, and they were both ready for the right person to settle down with.

Rebecca found the walls she had built crumbling gradually as she grew more and more comfortable with him as the evening wore on. He had an incredible way of making her laugh and had a sense of quiet repose. He also had an incredible collection of country classics including Johnny Cash, Waylon Jennings, Willie Nelson and Conway Twitty, just to name a few. Byron entertained her for hours as they sipped Jack Daniels and Coca Cola, danced with her, laughed with her, and played his guitar.

Taking her in his arms he slow danced with her to "Ring Of Fire" by Johnny Cash and her heart skipped a beat as he bent his head and caught her lips in a soft slow kiss. Pangs of desire swept through her pelvis as the kiss deepened and his probing tongue explored her willing mouth. Her arms went up around his neck instinctively and his hands slid down her back and pressed her hips into his. A soft moan escaped her lips as she felt him hard and hot against her.

"God you feel good!" Byron said huskily.

"So do you," she whispered softly.

Their embrace deepened and their breathing became heavier. Grabbing her hand, he led her to the master bedroom, to his bed where they lay side by side slowly exploring each other's body, shedding each other's clothes as they went along. As he lifted his head and gazed down at her, she suddenly had a thousand questions in her head.

"Will we be alright if we do this? Will we still look at each other with respect?"

"Of course we will. We are two adults and we know what we want. It is not the booze talking. All the Jack Daniels did was relax us, making us more comfortable with each other," Byron said, assuaging her fears and guilt. Lowering his head, he kissed her and gently fondled her breasts. Grasping a nipple between his thumb and forefinger, he rolled it gently back and forth until she was crying out for him. She reached down and he gasped with pleasure at the fire that spread though his loins with her touch. Rebecca marveled at the size of him, hard, hot, and throbbing with desire. Hot and wet she was ready for him.

As if reading her mind his hand slid down her stomach to the neat little triangle of hair between her legs. She instinctively opened her thighs as he slid a finger between her soft moist folds to the little button hidden within. Crying out in pleasure, she thrust her hips to meet his gentle strokes, knowing she was going to climax long before she wanted to. It had been months since a man had touched her and even longer since, it was pleasurable.

Byron's touch was unlike any she had ever experienced, as though she were the center of his complete attention. She slowed her hips to a very slow rocking motion to slow the oncoming orgasm but he did not seem to take her cue. Instead, he began to rotate the nub in a faster circular motion, picking up the rhythm instead of slowing it.

"Come on baby, I want to see you cum!"

"Oh Byron, it's too fast!" she gasped.

"So, you'll cum again. Trust me and go with it."

She did, she let loose, breathing rapidly and crying out his name as she thrust her hips to match his rhythm until she reached her peak. Her teeth clenched with the force of it as the orgasmic waves crashed over her and she reveled in the intensity of it, more intense than any she had ever experienced. As the waves ebbed, tears began to slide from beneath her eyelashes and a silent sob shook her body.

"Why are you crying sweetheart? What is wrong? Did I hurt you?"

"No! You did not hurt me! That was just the most intense orgasm I have ever experienced. It was like I became a part of you, and you knew where to touch me and exactly how."

"Hush little lady. That's just the beginning, you ain't seen anything yet!"

Pulling her close to him and tucking her into his broad shoulders he held her to him, breathing in her wonderful scent, reveling in her supple body. In a few moments, his heartbeat slowed, the blood flow to his groin abated, and he could relax against her.

"What about you?" she whispered, blushing a little.

"I'm fine dear. That was for you. I want to wait for the rest until the moment is perfect."

Feeling like she had cheated him a little, she snuggled closer to him and soon they drifted off to sleep.

CHAPTER 21

A warm wet tongue licking her mingled with soft little woofs awoke Angel on a still warm late summer morning. She laughed and hugged her little dog close to her chest. The sun was lighting up particles floating in the cabin air into glittering diamond dust. Pepper was full grown now, becoming her best friend and companion. She kissed him lovingly on his cold wet nose and hugged him gently to her neck.

Angels' imprisonment had become much more bearable since the arrival of Pepper. She talked to him about everything, her deepest fears, pains, worries, loneliness, and her momma... Pepper would whine and lick her hands and face, consoling her as if he understood every word she was saying. It had been over a year now and Angels' memory of her previous life had begun to fade. She still kept the image of her mother fresh in her mind daily, drawing several pictures of her so she could remember every detail of her mothers face. These were kept folded in half and tucked neatly inside her pillowcase.

Sitting up she reached outside the cage for some newspaper for Pepper to use the bathroom on. When he was finished, she placed the soiled paper in small garbage and tied it tightly. Squatting over a small basin she did her business, wiped, and then placed the lid back on the basin. She nearly gagged at the odor that wafted from the basin and assaulted her nostrils.

It was the third day since Robert had been to the cabin and

she found herself listening intently now for the sound of his tires in the gravel. Counting out Peppers food and filling his water dish she poured the last of the water into her plastic drinking glass. Removing the last two slices of bread from the bread bag she smeared a thick layer of peanut butter ort them and slowly ate them, washing the gooey stuff down with the last of her water.

Robert would be here today she thought to herself. He had never missed a day yet in the last fourteen months, showing up at least every third day to replenish her food and water supply. He had taught her to cook, clean, take care of herself, and her dog. She hated to admit it but she actually found herself looking forward to his arrivals now. She found she craved his attention now, even though it was painful at times.

Angel was learning arithmetic, geography, history, and spelling and had become quite adept at reading books intended for much older readers. The painful lessons he taught her she tolerated and had even learned to figure out quite fast how Robert wanted her to react to his tortures and pain, thus shortening the lessons. The last few months he had also begun to teach her communication and companionship. Robert was achieving his ultimate goal, which was to create the perfect female companion for his needs. Unbeknownst to Angel, she was falling right into the plan design he had created just for her. Angel was becoming exactly what his experiment was designed to create, and she was nearly ripe for the plucking.

She had finished the three books he had left her so she laid back on her pillow, placed Pepper on her stomach and began to review her spelling words that Robert would test her on later that day. She dozed off a while later waiting patiently for the sound of tires crunching gravel. As she slept, a snowy white feather fell softly from the rafters above the sleeping child as a guardian angel settled there to watch the child and her little companion sleep.

PART 3

TRUE LOVE CONQUERS EVIL

CHAPTER 22

S arah and Tyler sat at their dining room table. The entire table was covered with evidence involving Angel's case. The case was now officially a "cold case" but the captain had allowed them to copy the file and take it home, with the hope that his two best detectives could crack the case wide open. Half-empty cups of tepid coffee sat amid piles of notes, interviews, and photographs, in addition to all the lab reports. After several hours of pouring over the evidence, everything just seemed to jumble together and make little sense to either of them. Tyler sighed deeply and walked around the table to where Sarah was leaning over the table reading the report, her nicely rounded rump showing perfectly in her snug spandex running shorts.

Sneaking up behind her, he pressed his pelvis against the soft rounded object of his desire. Flexing her knees, she rubbed her rump up and down, hardening him in seconds and driving him near madness. Sliding the shorts slowly down he caressed her soft cheeks and then slid his hand down to the lips of her vagina and the little pleasure button hidden in it's folds. He found her clitoris already hardened and her lips moist with the dew of her desire, ready for his hard throbbing member. Unzipping his shorts, he slid his ready cock into her hot wet canal as he slid his finger from her folds.

Sarah gasped with sheer pleasure at his bold invasion of her womanhood and then bucked back against him impaling herself even farther onto his member. Thrusting heatedly backwards and forwards, they reached their climax simultaneously within minutes after which he lifted her into his arms and carried her upstairs. There he made love to her all over again, slower this time and with all the tenderness and affection, his heart could hold.

Afterward, they lay there locked in each other's arms, reveling at their good fortune in finding each other. They were completely and utterly compatible too, both loved adventure, country music, and work, hiking, camping fishing, and just having fun. They both lived life to its fullest because they dealt with so much death every day at work, both natural and unnatural, to want to waste one precious moment of life on ill feelings. Snuggling up against each other in the spoon position they both drifted off to sleep, their final thoughts of a beautiful, fair haired, blue-eyed Angel.

CHAPTER 23

Rebecca woke in the early hours of the day, Byron still wrapped around her. She had to go to the bathroom bad but she did not want to break the physical contact she had with him just yet. She played the previous night repeatedly in her mind and could not get over how tender and giving Byron had been. Not at all worried about his wants and desires, he had simply focused on her need for fulfillment.

Eventually her bladder won and she gently eased her body from beneath his, causing him to stir and turn onto his back, but after a few moments his soft snoring resumed which assured her he was still asleep. Tiptoeing, she made her way into the bathroom and relieved herself. Returning to his bed, she turned on her left side and lay there observing him.

"How handsome he is," she thought in wonder at her good fortune. Long blonde lashes lay against high cheekbones on a face worthy of being on a Greek god. He slept soundly, full lips slightly parted, his breathing deep and steady. She just could not get over the perfection of his face.

"How had she gotten so lucky or been chosen to have even this one beautiful night with such a wonderful man? Why he was not married to some gorgeous model or a beautiful wife? She knew he had a son, so what had happened to his first wife?" She knew from their conversations that he had just been through a two-year tumultuous relationship and was still on the rebound, as was she. Maybe it would work for them in spite of their emotional baggage, for now all she could do was hope.

A short time later Byron rolled over and threw his leg over hers, pulling her tightly into his chest at the same time. He was still half-asleep, but as he flexed his hips against her thigh, it was obvious that part of his body was wide-awake. He was rock hard and huge against her, the heat against her leg igniting her fires as well. A deep ache began in her pelvis and she felt the dew of desire damp between her legs, readying her secret place for him enter.

Deciding to treat him this time, she scooted down under the sheets and slid his Hanes down to free the throbbing member. She filled her mouth with as much of him as she could and slid her tongue rhythmically around the tip of his rod. Byron was now wide-awake and moaning with pleasure at her ministrations. His large hand grasped her upper arm and as she began to slide him up and down in her mouth, his grip tightening with the intensifying pleasure. Circling her hand around the base of the pulsing member, she stroked and sucked him in perfect rhythm. His body tensed and she felt her own climax building with his. Astounded at her bodies' reaction to his, she gave him all of her desire too and quickened the pace until he was groaning deep in his throat. She felt the ejaculate enter his penis and began to taste him, driving her even more. He tasted sweet and slightly salty; he actually tasted good to her taste buds. Their bodies exploded as one, both shuddering with the intensity of their orgasms.

Rebecca took his ejaculate in her mouth and swallowed it, without wanting to gag or vomit, unlike her experiences with Robert. The act she performed for Byron was one of her own accord, an act of total giving of her heart and body to please him. She discovered she enjoyed it immensely with Byron and was astounded that she had climaxed with him without physical stimulation. The fact that he tasted so good to her was just cream on the cake, an added bonus.

Rebecca realized as they held each other close that she was falling for this man. Falling hard and fast and a trickle of fear slid down her spine. She prayed fervently that he truly was the man he portrayed himself to be, and not a monster behind a handsome face like her ex.

CHAPTER 24

Little Angel awoke several hours later, the sun shining brightly through the grimy cabin windows. She guessed it was between two and three o'clock in the afternoon. Robert would arrive anytime in the next few hours. She made sure everything around the cage was neat and orderly, folding her blanket up neatly and placing it on her pillow. Then she brushed her long hair, damp from her sweating in the hot, airless cabin, put it in a ponytail and then cleaned the strands of hair from her hairbrush. Brushing her teeth and spitting into the urine basin, her stomach heaved at the sight and smell of its contents. Looking in her little plastic pocket mirror, a gift from Robert, she decided she looked as pretty as could be expected after her third day without a bath.

Scooping up her little furry friend, who she had named Pepper, she propped herself against her pillow and blanket and studied her vocabulary again, one ear tuned to hear the approaching of Roberts vehicle. About an hour later, she heard the telltale crunch of gravel under tires that signaled his arrival. The truck shut off and moments later, a truck door slammed, followed by keys grating in the three different deadbolts on the steel cabin door.

She had put Pepper down on the cage floor at the first sounds from the driveway and assumed the stance Robert had taught her, the one in which he was to be greeted. She sat primly with her lashes lowered, patiently awaiting his arrival indoors. The cabin door swung inward and Robert entered, sharp eyes scanning the cabin for signs of tampering. Satisfied his prisoner was still unfound he set several bags of groceries on the table, walked over to unlock the cage and set his little Angel free from her confining quarters. Climbing out of the cage, she gave Robert a gentle hug and a kiss on his stubbly cheek, grateful for his company.

"How's my little Angel?"

"Fine" she replied in a strong steady voice, no longer in fear of her captor,

"Good, we are going to make beef stroganoff tonight. Another of my favorites I wish to teach you to make for me."

"Okay, that sounds great" she said with a small smile, careful to show just the right amount of emotion.

Setting the groceries out of the bag onto the counter, they worked together preparing the meal. The teacher and the all too attentive student who was falling into the role he wanted her to, much to his silent elation. The night went well, her lessons were bearable and she aced her vocabulary and math tests, eager of late to please her master. Robert showed his pride in her progress with small hugs and very few words of praise. Angel ate up the small tokens of appreciation and affection, as he was her only human contact and her only contact with the outside world, which was now like a fading memory deep in her mind.

By the time he left, her food and water were replenished, she had bathed under his brooding gaze, the cabin was spotless, and her dog's supplies stocked as well. With a small hug and a kiss goodbye, he locked her back in her little prison and bid her goodnight. After a few moments of sitting in silence after the door was locked and the truck engine faded, Pepper whined and licked her cheek where a solitary tear traced its way down her forlorn face. Picking him up, she curled up in a ball with him in her arms and was soon fast asleep. It was a sleep filled with nightmares and dreamscapes. Nightmares where Robert never came back, where she and Pepper were left to starve to death in their cage. Dreamscapes of her mother laughing and playing with them in the park mingled with the nightmares. Another was of a beautiful white angel flying around the cabin, moonlight shimmering from a golden sword in its right hand.

CHAPTER 25

Tyler awoke before dawn from a strange dream. It was a dream about a hunting accident he had investigated a while back. He had closed the case ruling the death accidental. The man had been shot through the femoral artery with a shot from a 410-hunting rifle. In Tyler's dream, the man was laying on the autopsy table in the local morgue. Tyler was examining the autopsy notes from the chief medical examiner and comparing it with his investigation. Suddenly the man opened his eyes and spoke to him.

"I was murdered in cold blood" spoke the corpse.

Tyler's jaw dropped as he was completely taken aback by the talking dead.

"Who did this to you?" he questioned of the living dead.

"Robert Wilson" the corpse replied and then as quickly as he had arisen from the dead, Terry Alexander slipped into his decaying state once more.

Sweating, heart pounding, Tyler awoke and stared up at the ceiling for a while, attempting to decipher his dream. Rolling on his side, he gazed, down at his sleeping wife who was breathing deeply with a soft snore. Brushing her hair from her brow, he lowered his mouth to place a feather light kiss there. She smiled softly in her sleep but did not wake. Deciding suddenly not to wake his mate, he slid quietly from the bed, slipped on his robe and made his way out to the dining room. He opened the top drawer of his file cabinet in the dining room turned office and thumbed through the A's to Alexander. Inside the file were his personal notes from the investigation and a copy of the medical examiners autopsy report and ruling on the death. Taking the file, he quietly walked into the kitchen and put a pot of coffee on to brew.

Opening the file, he spread its contents and photos across the table, categorizing them by levels of evidence. Interviews from the man's wife and family had revealed that forty-seven year old Terry Alexander had been an avid hunter since the age of sixteen. His wife and grown children could not believe that Terry had entered the woods without the protection of his orange hunting overalls, bright orange vest and hat.

"He was always adamant about hunters wearing their colors and being careful out there in the woods," she had stated. In addition, her two sons and three daughters all agreed on the same thing. According to his children, their father would never enter the woods without having been fully dressed out in hunters orange.

"So what was he doing out there dressed in camouflage?" Tyler mussed to himself. He could find nothing in the autopsy to indicate the man had been doing drugs, or otherwise under the influence of any chemical agents. Nor was there any evidence to show whether the man had been drinking or otherwise disoriented. The body had been exposed to the elements too long to determine these facts. One thing he had learned in his years of investigations was that human beings are creatures of habit. For some reason Terry had abandoned his own safety rules and hunting habits, ironically, he had wound up dead because of it.

"Or was there another explanation for his death?" the seasoned investigator asked himself. He had failed to catch the irony in his original overview of the reports. Now Terry had haunted him in his dreams..

"To acquire what?" Tyler mused to himself. "Justice? Had he

really been murdered and Tyler's subconscious mind had finally sensed the irony? On the other hand, had the dead mans soul really come to him and demanded justice? And what connection could Robert Wilson possibly have had to Terry Alexander?"

CHAPTER 26

Byron lay on a bearskin rug in front of his fireplace; Rebecca snuggled in his arms, her back to his chest. They had spent the evening cooking and then cleaning up the kitchen. Afterward, they sipped Jack Daniels and Pepsi while dancing to classic country legends. Slowly, tentatively, she opened up her soul and out poured her life story. All the while, she was terrified he would pull away from her, blame her somehow for her horrific life, and she would lose the friend and lover she had just acquired.

Tears flowed softly down her cheeks as she spoke, detailing the injustices she had experienced. Beginning back at age four when a cousin had molested her in the church basement until the present she had been molested, abused, beaten, physically and emotionally battered as well.

She told of her son who she had lost to a drunk driver and all the turmoil that had caused for years. Finally, she arrived at the juncture of her life where Robert came into play. Robert had been the worst monster of them all, the one man who had shattered her inside. He stole her self-confidence, self-esteem, faith, trust, and pride until she hardly recognized who she had become anymore.

Byron had helped her put the final changes on her recovery. Therapy had helped bring her back to the woman she used to be, it had helped heal the wounds on her heart. The scars festered now and again and that would fade in time but probably remain the rest of her life. This newfound friend and wonderful, patient, understanding person was helping her progress to a full recovery.

He tightened his arm around her belly and pulled her tighter into the masculine strength of his body, her head cradled in the crook of his arm. Reaching up he wiped the tears from her eyes and face.

"It's okay Rebecca, I'm not going to hurt you or desert you. What kind of asshole would I be if I did that? You are not to blame for the pain and injustices you have suffered. Especially those that Robert inflicted on you. All you did was love him; he did not deserve a woman as beautiful as you are. Most men dream of discovering a mate with a heart such as yours. Roberts's sins are his own to be accountable for." Little did he realize at that time just how many sins Robert had committed against Rebecca and her little lost child.

"I thank God that I was at the hospital that day and met you. You brought hope back to my own heart."

"You really mean that?" she asked, voice quivering with emotion.

"Yes, I don't lie and I think I'm falling in love with you."

"Me too" she whispered softly, reaching up and touching his face with her fingertips.

Clutching her hand to his mouth he kissed every fingertip, then he started with her lips, then neck, ears, and down between her ample breasts as he lifted her shirt over her head. Flicking his tongue at each nipple he suckled at them until her breath was ragged gasps. He let his tongue travel the valley between her breast and down her taut belly to her little dip signaling her belly button. Here he drove her to an even greater level of excitement as he explored the little innie until he himself was hard and hot with need.

Slowly he unbuttoned her jeans and she raised her hips for him to slide them down and then let him pull them off one leg at a time. Byron then resumed the attention his tongue had been giving her, from her slender waist down to the neatly, closely trimmed patch that accented her womanhood. Hot and wet with desire she began to thrust her hips upward towards his eager flicking tongue that was driving her to that upward spiral that would lead to her climax. Tasting her damp, salty ocean of desire and knowing it was all for him, a low moan escaped him.

Kneeling between her legs, he perused her beautiful body. From her dark softly curling hair, high cheekbones, soft full lips now parted with her own moans of desire. Smoky green eyes caressed her full, still firm breasts, flat, taut stomach, long beautiful legs, toned thighs and calves, and finally to her perfect size seven feet. Instinctively, she spread her legs and he felt a jolt of desire go through him as he gazed upon her womanhood, glistening with love dew and soft pink in the firelight. Placing his hands, one under each firm buttock, he held her steady as his tongue tasted and explored her sweet feminine folds, his desire mounting as moans of pleasure escaped her and her whole body quivered with desire.

At last, he could hold back no more and he reached down, releasing his shaft from its confines. Byron sensed her mounting desire and knew she was close to the brink of ecstasy as he slid inside her warm folds. She was gloriously tight and hot, wet with the juices of her desire. She gasped and clasped her legs around his waist as he filled her, filled her completely, almost painfully, as he began to thrust deeper and deeper into her.

Nails raked his back as she clung to him, rocking her hips to match his rhythm, stroke for stroke as they quickly rode the waves of their desire to the ultimate goal. Then, simultaneously, the world shattered around them into millions of scintillating stars as they achieved ecstasy as one.

CHAPTER 27

The hot late summer sun beat down on the little cabin in the woods. Angel awoke to Pepper licking her face and whining. Yawning, she stretched, her feet pressing against the hard cool metal of the cage door, rattling the padlock momentarily. She was getting bigger and now she had to bend her knees to keep the hard metal of the cage door from pressing against her feet as she slept. Pepper had to do his business and was hungry. Sitting up, the top of her head nearly touched the roof of the cage. She was nearly nine years old now she noted as she glanced at the small calendar taped to the side of the cage. It was only one more month until her birthday. "What would Robert do for her birthday?" she wondered.

Fixing Peppers paper, she filled his small bowl with dry food, the bag nearly empty afterwards. Robert would be there today sometime she smiled to herself with anticipation. Robert's arrival meant a bath, fresh food and water, a clean urine basin, and human contact. Angel finished her morning routine of feeding Pepper and herself then cleaning up after them both. After brushing her teeth and hair, she made sure everything was tidy and clean. Bored, she leaned back on her pillow to finish her latest book "Gone with the Wind." She read until the sun was high in the sky and her stomach rumbled with hunger. The cabin had become hot and stuffy inside. She ate her last couple peanut butter crackers and washed them down regretfully with her last half a glass of water. It may be hours yet before Robert showed with water and it promised to h a sweltering day inside the airless cabin.

The days were long and hot now and she had learned to ration her water so she would not run out early but the last two days had been almost unbearably hot. She had given Pepper more than usual also due to his panting and whining from the heat. Odors from the urine and feces bucket were also much stronger than usual and when she squatted to use the bucket, the odor actually burned her sensitive nostrils. Lying back on her pillow and blanket, she soon dozed off, the heat making her extremely drowsy.

CHAPTER 28

Sarah walked into the kitchen a few hours after Tyler with her fleece robe on, hair rumpled and eyes bleary from sleep.

"Coffees nearly gone already?" she said kissing him good morning. "How long have you been up, husband?"

"Oh since about four thirty a.m. dear wife" he replied kissing her back. "Sorry about the coffee, I'll pour you the last cup and put another on to brew."

"I'll get it honey; you look like you've had a rough morning. "What's going on?"

"I had a strange dream last night. Do you remember that hunter that was found last spring up in Clinton County?"

"Yeah, vaguely. Didn't you rule the case as an accidental shooting?"

"Yeah" Tyler sighed wearily, "but last night he came to me in a dream. He was lying on the autopsy table and he opened his eyes and told me he had been murdered. Then, to make it even weirder, he told me that Robert Wilson killed him. When I came down and pulled the file on it I discovered some discrepancies I had not noticed before, probably because we were so tied up with Angel's case. If Robert killed him then the period would have been right around the time of Angel's disappearance. It could be the clue that turns this case around. It would almost have to be linked to Angel, if Robert did indeed kill Terry."

"My God, you are right" Sarah said, adrenaline beginning to trickle from her brain, raising her heart rate just a bit. "Maybe he had Terry kidnap Angel and then killed him to be sure no one ever connected the two of them. Can you imagine what this could mean? We could finally solve Angel's case and link it directly to Robert. God, I hope there's some evidence left out there that can positively connect him to Robert!"

"Yeah, me too" replied Tyler. "I should have been more thorough over a year ago when I reviewed the case. Because of my failure to connect it, the case was not solved a long time ago. And God only knows what I'm responsible for when it comes to Angel and Rebecca's pain."

"Now Tyler, please don't go and blame yourself. You are a great investigator but you are not God. You cannot read a dead mans mind any more than a live ones. Let us get showered and go down to the station and pull the original files and evidence. Let's see if there's anything solid we can find to at least point suspicion in Robert's direction." An hour later, they climbed into Tyler's SUV and headed for the station. Sarah's arms filled with notebooks they had both collected on the case.

CHAPTER 29

Rebecca was moving the last of her things into Byron's home when the phone rang.

"Hello" she answered in a breathless voice.

"Rebecca?"

"Yes."

"Hi, this is Sarah."

"Hello Sarah" Rebecca said, her heart dropping to her knees as she sank to the floor with the phone to her ear.

"Rebecca, I don t want to upset you or get your hopes up, but we seem to have had a break in the case. Could you come down here to the station and talk with us?"

"Sure, when do you want me to come?"

"As soon as you possibly can," Sarah replied with an empathetic voice. "I know you're still in the middle of moving, but this is very important.

"I'll be right down" Rebecca answered quickly. Dialing Byron's number as she climbed into her Blazer, Rebecca headed for the police station.

"Hello sweetheart" Byron's deep voice answered almost immediately.

"Sarah called. I have to go to the station and talk to them because they have had a break in the case. Maybe they'll find my baby," she said excitedly.

"Calm down sweetheart. I do not want you to get you are

95

hopes up too much and set yourself up to be disappointed. If you need to talk, call me. I am sorry I cannot be right there with you but remember my thoughts are with you. Do not forget too, I love you with all my heart. And honey, please let me know as soon as you find out anything. I pray they find her and that she's okay, I told you I always wanted a little girl."

"I know and I love you too," Rebecca said softly. "I'll be alright and I promise I'll call and fill you in as soon as soon as I know what's going on." A short while later she was sitting in Sarah and Tyler's office where they carefully detailed Tyler's dream and the evidence they had since uncovered.

"Did you know that Robert had a half brother named Terry Alexander?" Tyler began the questions.

"No, I know his other two brothers but they were full blood brothers all from the same mother and father."

"Well, apparently Robert's father had an affair with a younger woman by the name of Leslie Alexander when Robert was a young boy of seven or eight. The relationship ended quickly due to Robert's mother discovering the mistress. She apparently ran the young woman out of town, but not before she became pregnant" Sarah began the story.

"The woman gave birth in another state and although she gave Terry her last name she still placed Robert's father on the birth certificate. Years later, he attempted to discover his father but he was dead. In the search process, he met Robert, his half brother, because Robert bore his father's name. About a year ago, Terry Alexander's body was discovered in the woods of Clinton County. The discovery and subsequent investigation was initially closed as a hunting accident.

Then came Tyler's dream and we re-opened the case. Upon further questioning of his widow, we discovered that Terry had recently found one of his half-brothers. This was the break we had been searching and praying to find. Terry was murdered and his body disposed of right about the same period of Angel's disappearance. We have questioned all of Terry's family and friends and none had ever heard Angel's name mentioned by Terry. It is our beliefs that Robert had Terry kidnap Angel for him and then killed Terry because it was the only way to connect them all together.

Top surveillance equipment is in place as well as a wiretap and GPS locator as we finally had enough evidence to persuade a judge to allow it. If Angel is still alive we will find her, I assure you of that" Sarah finished adamantly.

Tyler picked the conversation up at that point to reassure Rebecca. "We will keep you abreast of every move we make and every step of the investigation from here to the end. I am only sorry I missed the link earlier, who knows what might have happened."

"It's okay Tyler," Rebecca said. "I know both of you have done your best and I know that Robert is an evil, vile, despicable, sorry excuse of a man!"

CHAPTER 30

A tiny red light flashed on the computer screen. Robert was moving. The first two days had yielded nothing except his trips to work and the local gym. Today however, he went to the gym early and then left his home again at 4:10 p.m. They watched the little red beacon drive through town and then stop at a local Wal-Mart. Their spirits fell once more. It had been over a year since the kidnapping, and they feared little Angel was gone. For an hour, the flashing light did not move and then suddenly the light moved again. Instead of heading towards home, the light headed for the mountains of Center Pennsylvania.

Breathlessly they watched it progress into Clinton County way out on Rte 144. Half way between Clarence Pa. and Renovo Pa. it turned left into a wild game reserve onto a road called Jews Run Road. Tyler grabbed the phone as pieces of the puzzle clicked into place. He vaguely recalled Terry's widow saying something about a hunting camp of Robert's where Terry was told he could hunt. He had never made it there, as far as she knew. Tyler knew he had made it there, he also knew that Terry had never made it home afterward.

Tyler mobilized his units and the few sharpshooters he had on his force. He phoned the captain and Sarah and she arrived fifteen minutes later to make the long ride. Donning their Kevlar vests, they climbed into their four-wheel drive Jeep Grand Cherokee used for off road investigations and headed for the mountains, adrenaline already pumping through their veins. Several other vehicles trailed behind them carrying the rest of his team and all the protective gear, CSI equipment, and ammunition they may need. Pulling off at a granite boulder marking the left turn that would be Jews Run, Tyler assembled his men for instructions and words of inspiration.

"Okay men, we will take him at the top of the hill. There are pull offs halfway up and at the very top. When he passes the first pull off, halfway up the trail, we will pull a vehicle onto the road to prevent him from attempting to back up and make a run for it. We will pull out in front of him just as he tops the hill. He will be blocked in; there is no way for him to turn off the frail without landing his truck in a ditch. Remember he is armed and very dangerous. He has killed at least once before men, however. I would wager to guess many times. Please do not try to be heroes. Let us do this quickly and professionally with little or no bloodshed. We have the element of surprise on our side and we need to take him alive if at all possible in case Angel is not at the cabin."

The units disappeared quickly and quietly, melting into the thick underbrush of the mountainside. The sky was cloudy with no moonlight, giving the vehicles added protection from Robert's sight. They waited for nearly three hours, however, when Tyler's voice whispered over the airwaves, a burst of adrenaline shot through them bringing them fully alert.

"Heads up men, he's on the way up the hill!" Tyler said evenly and with authority, although, in his chest his heart was racing. He fought to control his emotions and keep steadily focused on the job at hand. Trigger fingers were steady and patient as the officers waited, watching the headlights cut through the darkness. Slowly, the vehicle wound its way from the valley below up the steep mountainside to where the officers were hidden.

Robert's mind drifted and fantasized about Angel as he drove the rutted, rugged trail to the top. He was totally oblivious to the officers waiting for him. He had become complacent in his journey to and from Angel as the months had progressed. He no longer checked for vehicles behind him once he left the city limits, nor did he inspect his vehicle for tracking devices anymore. For the first year, he had been extremely thorough but as time wore on, he relaxed in the idea that he was in the clear. He was so adept at getting away with murder he now thought of himself as invincible. The interviews and questions had ceased and Terry had been found months ago, his death ruled accidental, besides that, he had left no connection to himself and Terry. Thus, he became careless and overly confident in the commission of his crimes.

Robert couldn't possibly know it, but in the next few minutes his entire plan for Angel was about to unravel. Tyler watched Robert's approaching him and then gunned his Jeep forward onto the road, blocking any attempt to escape the man might try. Robert saw the Jeep and, as predicted, slammed on his brakes and threw the vehicle into reverse. Churning gravel, he attempted to head backwards down the hill. Catching sight of the vehicle blocking his dissent, he floored the gas and slammed into it, sending his pickup into a skid.

As if in slow motion, the truck spun gravel and then slid sideways off the road and into a deep ditch. The nose of the pickup was in the air and officers moved swiftly from their places in the underbrush to the truck. Yanking open the drivers door, they hauled Robert out and ordered him to the ground. He lay prone in the gravel, a dozen automatic handguns targeted on his head lest he should attempt to get up. Tyler sauntered up and frisked Robert, removing a handgun from his ankle holster and another from his back waistband. Task complete, he placed his booted right foot on Roberts's neck, applying just enough pressure to show he was serious.

"Where is she?"

"I don't know who you're talking about. Who is she?" Robert

replied, feigning innocence.

The pressure of the boot heel on his neck increased and the "teacher of strength'" the "right hand of God" bawled like a baby.

"She's in the cabin! I didn't hurt her!"

"Yes you did, you pervert, every day since you had her kidnapped from her mother you have hurt her!" Tyler growled at him, fire in his eyes. "I hope you get the chair for killing Terry and I hope they rape and torture you every night until you are put to death. Sarah, come here and speak your peace, you've been working as hard as I have and deserve at least that satisfaction," Tyler said, motioning to his wife.

"You know what Tyler, I hope they spare his life and he spends every minute of the rest of his life behind bars. We all know what happens to child molesters and women beaters in prison. They become real men's bitches and they get it up the ass every night with broomsticks and bottles, among many other torturous objects," Sarah finished, glaring down into Roberts one visible eye.

Tyler motioned for his officers and they hauled him to his feet, shackled his hands and feet, and threw him into the back of one of the SUVs used for transport. Sarah and Tyler stood close together for a moment, letting the rush of the capture subside as the vehicle carrying the human scum faded into the black night.

CONCLUSION

Angel lay in her cage, belly full, freshly bathed, quiet and content. She missed Robert already, though he had only been gone a short while. On the floor just outside her cage of terror, her eyes caught sight of a small white feather. Picking it up, she tickled her face with its softness while pondering where it had come from. Looking up towards the rafters, she saw only shadows in the dark cabin but in the soft moonlight, she thought she could make out a great white bird perched in the rafters. Rubbing her eyes, she looked again. The winged creature still appeared to be there, however it was so still and deathly quiet that she decided it had been only her imagination.

She tickled her nose with the feather and giggled, suddenly feeling at peace, then placed it in her pillowcase with the drawings she had hidden there. Picking up her furry white companion, she tucked Pepper in her arms and within moments, they fell fast asleep. A short time later, Pepper whined and tires crunching in the gravel drive suddenly awakened her. Her heart began to pound and Pepper continued to whine. Robert had come back.

"Why?" she wondered with fear filling her heart and soul. Something had to be wrong because Robert never came back. A second vehicle approached just as she heard the doors of the first one slamming shut and fear filled her physical body. She began to shake uncontrollably.

"Should she scream?" she wondered. "Was it someone who could save her, or was it Robert bringing back the man she so vividly recalled kidnapping her from the park?" Suddenly, someone was knocking at the door and calling out her name.

"Angel, Angel, are you in there?" called a woman's voice.

"Angel, if you're in there let us know, we are the police and are here to help you," stated a kind male voice. Survival instincts kicked in as hope soared through Angel's soul. Someone had found her!

Help, help me please!" the child screamed at the top of her lungs.

"Open the door for us if you can," said the female cop.

"I can't open the door" she screamed back, "I'm locked in a cage!"

"Hold on Angel, we'll get you out!" yelled the kind male voice. Moments later a battering ram struck the door and on the third strike, the door gave way with a crash. SWAT officers swarmed into the cabin first to make sure it was clear and no traps had been set. Tyler and Sarah were given the thumbs up and they entered the little cabin. Their hearts broke at the sight before them, a beautiful angelic child locked in a dog kennel in the middle of a meager cabin. For nearly two years she had lived in the cage, and God knew what other horrors Robert had bestowed upon her.

Quickly, they cut the padlock from the cage door and freed the child, clutched in her arms, a little white dog. When they tried to remove the animal, she tightened her grip on the dog and refused to let them take it from her. After determining her general health was all right, in spite of her pale skin and shivering uncontrollably, they put a blanket around her. She said nothing, but Angel was not shivering from the cold, but from anxiety and fear. She could remember very little about her life before Robert.

"Robert is in jail" spoke the woman softly. "Your mother is at the station waiting on you. Would you like to go and see her?"

Nodding emphatically she took the woman's hand and was led to a waiting vehicle. Sarah tucked Angel and her furry companion into the back seat and then climbed in beside her. She held little Angel in her arms as Tyler drove the girl out of the forest and away from her long nightmare. Sarah looked back at the cabin as Tyler pulled away and in the dark shadow of the cabin, she swore she saw a great white bird take flight towards the starry sky. A smile played across her lips as she remembered Tyler's dream that had led them to rescue Angel. Placing her hand on the child's fair hair, she silently thanked God for the guardian angel He had sent to protect this most innocent of victims. Settling back into the seat, protective motherly arms wrapped around the girl, they settled in for the long ride back to the station. Back to a new life for the little one, and to her eagerly awaiting mother and stepfather to be.

ΔΔΔ

CPSIA information can be obtained at www.ICGtesting.com
231149LV00002B/4/P